Her husband was dead, how could she go on?

Sarah took Frankie to school and then went to her job at the CPA's office. After work, she retrieved Frankie from school, picked up a few items at the grocery store, and went home to start supper. It was seven o'clock and Frank had not come home from work. He said he had a long day, so Sarah was not worried.

When the phone rang, Sarah got a deep feeling of dread. "Hello," she said, and there was a pause. She suddenly felt like she had been hit with a rock, then she dropped the phone and fell to the floor.

"What's wrong, Momma?" Frankie yelled and ran to her. He shook her and picked her head up off the floor, weeping profusely, still shaking her, trying to wake her up.

Frank Ross's car had been blinded-sided by a pickup truck being driven by a drunk driver. Sarah's husband, the love of her life and the father of her son, was dead at twenty-nine years of age.

When Frank Ross met Sarah Mayeux in high school, it was love at first sight. Little did she know when she married him, however, that fate had deemed the worst-case scenario for her, that she would lose her husband before they had a chance to grow old. Clayton Conner has loved Sarah for years and feels her pain, especially since he is now married to a woman he doesn't love and not free to make his feelings for Sarah known. Sarah's son, Frankie, and Clayton's daughter, Addy, always thought they would grow up and get married. Then Addy meets someone else in college, and Frankie is devastated. But fate isn't any kinder to them. Each married to someone else, they discover too late just how wrong their choices were. Will fate intervene with these star-crossed lovers, or are they all doomed to be unhappy forever?

KUDOS for *False River*

In *False River* by Jack Sprouse, Sarah Mayeux falls in love with Frank Ross in high school and several lives are changed forever. The story follows Frank and Sarah and their children as well as the Connor family, Sarah's old boyfriend who never got over her. As tragedies and loss affect the families, each member is forced to make hard decisions and examine past choices. Never an easy thing to do. A touching and inspiring story of love, loss, and starting over. ~ *Taylor Jones, The review Team of Taylor Jones & Regan Murphy*

False River by Jack Sprouse is the story of a young couple in New Roads, Louisiana. Sarah and Frank fall in love in high school, even though Sarah is dating someone else at the time. When Sarah gets pregnant, Frank quickly marries her, fulfilling the promise he made her the first time he met her. Frank and Sarah have a son, Frankie, who grows up in New Roads. Frankie falls in love with Addy Connor, the daughter of Sarah's old boyfriend, but fate has other plans for them and life is not kind. *False River* is a story of choices, some good and some not so good, and how those choices can affect our lives and the lives of those we love. Heartwarming and poignant. ~ *Regan Murphy, The review Team of Taylor Jones & Regan Murphy*

ACKNOWLEDGMENTS

I would like to thank my granddaughter. Cheyenne Victoria Middleton, for the beautiful cover art.

Other Books by

Jack Sprouse

And

Black Opal Books

Clare

Magnolia Road

Dreams Once Dreamed

A Bowl Full of Grapes

The House Wren

FALSE RIVER

JACK SPROUSE

A Black Opal Books Publication

GENRE: HISTORICAL ROMANCE/FAMILY/WOMEN'S FICTION

This is a work of fiction. Names, places, characters and incidents are either the product of the author's imagination or are used fictitiously, and any resemblance to any actual persons, living or dead, businesses, organizations, events or locales is entirely coincidental. All trademarks, service marks, registered trademarks, and registered service marks are the property of their respective owners and are used herein for identification purposes only. The publisher does not have any control over or assume any responsibility for author or third-party websites or their contents.

DEDICATION

This book is dedicated to my wife, Barbara,
who was born in New Roads, Louisiana

Table of Contents

PROLOGUE

The people who lived in New Roads, Louisiana, as did people who lived in any scenic locale, rarely took notice of the natural beauty of the small town and its environs. Caught up in the daily grind of life, love, responsibilities, and obligations, it was most likely true that few of them ever indulged themselves in quiet, pensive, appreciation of the pleasant little town. The mighty oaks and pecan orchards that graced the stretches of road along Louisiana's Route 1 provided shade and comfort and images of the Old South. The town was laid out along the banks of False River, called False River, after the Mississippi River changed course in 1722 and left a lake, where once The Big Muddy, had flowed.

The little town was a microcosm of contrasting de-
mographics. Small, two-bedroom, wood frame houses,
lined most of the streets extending away from Main
Street. They had, in latter days, begun to be interspersed
with more attractive homes, having garages, patios, and
landscaped yards. It was a side-effect of creeping afflu-
ence and the influx of vacation-home owners from Baton
Rouge and New Orleans, who had built million-dollar
homes across Main Street on the river side. Boat houses
and docks dotted the shoreline on both sides of the river,
and piers jutted out into the river, from which people
fished and gained access to watercraft.

Frank Robert "Frankie" Ross had little inclination to
contemplate the scenery afforded him by the warm
greenery and sparkling blue water of his home town and
its magnificent lake. Frankie's life had been hard after his
father died, when Frankie was twelve years old, in a car
wreck. Frank Ross had been returning from his job in Baton Rouge.

The Ross family lived in a house on Janis, "Jah-
neese" Street, as it was pronounced by the locals. In the
four years since his father's death, Frankie's mother, Sarah, worked as a waitress in a very popular local restaurant to support herself and her only child. It was hard
work, and Sarah often came home so exhausted that she
could not devote much time to Frankie.

Frankie was now eighteen and about to graduate
from high school. Summer was upon him and, unlike

most of his friends, Frankie expected to work all summer. For many, it would be a hiatus before beginning their college careers, preparing them for their future lives and greater things.

Frankie had no future, except for that which was encompassed by a diminutive, beautiful, girl named Adeline Connor. Her parents called her Adeline but, to the world outside the Connor home, she was Addy. Addy had brown hair that fell just below her ears. Captivating dark brown eyes, so dark they almost looked black, drew admiring comments from boys and men, and women, as well. She often wore her hair with one side pushed behind her ear. Pearl-drop earrings were her only accoutrements, save, a smile that could light up a crowded room or a broken heart.

Frankie first became aware of Addy when they were in elementary school. Addy had a crush on Frankie and the two became friends, despite their families being on opposite sides of the economic scale in new Roads. The Connors were well off, and the Rosses were not.

By the time they were in high school, Frankie was in love with Addy Connor. He was a senior and she was in her junior year at Rosenwald high school in New Roads, and he believed that he would never stop loving her.

CHAPTER 1

Sarah

The ceremony was over, and everyone had left. Two men stood by, a short distance from the canopy, waiting respectfully, to cover the grave. They were careful not to disturb the lady, sitting alone with the young boy.

She was spending a few final moments with whoever was in the casket. She held an American flag, given to her by the men from the VFW, who had been pall bearers for her husband.

The two men spoke quietly to each other, not wanting to appear to be rushing her. "He was a Vietnam veteran," one of them said, and the other man nodded. "Woman left alone with a young-un, ain't nuthin but another sad story."

Sarah had no tears left, she had spent them all, and her mind began to wander.

ೕೂೕ

It was 1967, Poydras High School, the year they would be graduating. Frank Ross was the cutest boy in town, according to Sarah Mayeux, and most of her friends. Frank had a wild side that was only tempered by the five-foot-four-inch, green-eyed beauty.

"Do you have a boyfriend?" were the first words he ever spoke to her, the first day of the school year.

"Yes," was her response, "sort of," she added.

"What does 'sort of' mean?" he asked.

"I've been dating a college guy."

"Well, you're going to have to forget him," Frank said.

"I am," she replied, "and why do I have to do that? He's a nice guy."

"Because I love you, and we're going to get married."

Sarah started giggling. "You're just a wee bit full of yourself, aren't you?"

"So, I've been told," he said, "let's go to the movies on Saturday, and we can discuss this."

"What if I have plans on Saturday?"

"You have to change them," he told her. "Do you have plans on Saturday?"

"Not really," she said, "but you don't even know my name."

"What is your name?" he asked.

"I'm Sarah Mayeux," she said, "who are you?"

"Frank Ross is my name," he replied. His demeanor became slightly less abrasive. He took her hand in his and kissed it then held it in both of his. "I'm sorry, Sarah Mayeux. Maybe I came on a little too strong, but you're the prettiest girl I've ever seen, and I really would like to take you to the movies. Can you change your plans?"

"Where did you come from?"

"Baton Rouge," he said, "I came here this past summer to stay with my dad. I grew up in New Roads, but I left with my mom when she divorced my dad.

"Where do you live?" she asked him.

"My dad has a house on Janis Street," he said, pronouncing the street name like it is spelled.

"It's Jah-neese Street, not Janis," she corrected him.

"Oh, right, I think I heard that before. My dad calls it that. I thought it was just him, but I guess not."

"So, tell me again why you love me," she said.

"I don't know why, Sarah Mayeux, I just know I do. You're going to have to marry me."

"Well, if we are going to get married, then I suppose we had better go to a movie, and maybe see if you can figure out why you love me. But first, you're going to have to stop calling me by both my names, just call me Sarah." At this point, she was enjoying her humoring of the brash boy from Baton Rouge, figuring he was just trying to get her off her feet.

"I can do that," he said.

Frank had lived with his mother in Baton Rouge since his parents' divorce when he was ten years old. It had been a bitter separation that Frank never comprehended. He had only seen his father during the summers, and occasionally when he had come to Baton Rouge to visit the boy.

With the passing of his mother, during the summer of 1967, when Frank was eighteen, he came to live with his dad in New Roads. He started his final year in school at Poydras High, and that was when he saw Sarah. His life would never be the same again. A looming problem hung over his head, however, which he had not told her about. Frank had joined the army reserve when he turned seventeen. In 1969, with the Vietnam War raging, it was only a matter of time before he would have to go on active duty and, almost certainly, be sent to Vietnam.

Sarah fell in love with Frank, and no one was more surprised than she when it happened. He never faltered in his love for her, and he asked her to marry him before the end of the school year. She had been dating a local boy from town, but he was in college at LSU and only came home on the weekends. The college *man* had made his love for her apparent and wanted to marry her when she got out of high school. She would have a future and a good life with Clayton Conner, and she could make a good case for dismissing this brash and bold braggart, Frank Ross. But he had kissed her hand in the hallway at school and kissed her in the King Theater that following Saturday. Something happened deep inside her, when he kissed her.

"If you really love me, like you say you do, then I will marry you, Frank," she told him.

"I do love you, Sarah," he promised her. "I know, when I came on to you so strong, you thought I was just wanting to get in your pants, which I was." She started giggling, and he continued, "But I wasn't lying. I really did fall for you the first time I saw you."

In March of 1969, Sarah discovered that she was pregnant. She was reluctant to tell Frank, at first, for fear that he might change his mind about wanting to marry her. Her folks were distraught and, being older people, they were stricken with the fear that they might have to raise the baby themselves. Their concern for their daughter did not match their concern for the *family name*. They wanted to send her somewhere to have the baby, on the misguided notion that her fall from grace could be kept a secret from a small town like New Roads."

"We'll get married now," Frank insisted, "don't worry about what people might think or say. This is the happiest day of my life. We'll live with my dad until I can get us a place."

"I was afraid you wouldn't want to marry me when I told you I was pregnant."

"I told you I love you, Sarah. I meant it," he said.

They named the boy Frank Robert, not his father's middle name, because Frank Ross didn't want to saddle his son with being called Junior. They called the boy Frankie.

Two months after the baby boy was born, Frank got the call from the army. Frank had his pay sent home to Sarah, saving only enough for himself for minimum living expenses. Sarah visited the local Catholic Church every day and prayed for God to bring Frank back to her, alive and in one complete piece. She never wavered from her daily ritual.

Just before he was scheduled for R & R, Frank Ross's unit was ordered to join American forces already engaged in Operation Texas Star, in the A Shau Valley and the mountains east of the valley. The purpose of the operation was to regain the initiative in the area Fought between April first and September fifth, 1970, the operation culminated in the Battle of Fire Support Base Ripcord.

The Battle of Fire Support Base Ripcord was a twenty-three-day battle between elements of the army's 101st airborne division and two reinforced divisions of the North Vietnamese Army, from July first to July twenty-second, 1970. It was the last major confrontation between US ground forces and the North Vietnamese Army.

As part of second battalion, of the 506th infantry division, Frank's platoon became engaged in hostilities in the A Shau Valley in support of Fire Support Base Ripcord. After the helicopter insertion, they took up positions in the jungle covered hills surrounding the base. His unit was part of the overall effort to interdict resupply traffic of the 6th NVA Regiment, along the Ho Chi Minh Trail. The platoon leader was an inexperienced second lieutenant named Melton.

Melton was not without merit. However, he was intelligent and a quick learner. But he had only been in Vietnam for less than three months and this was his first assignment as a platoon commander. The real leader of the unit and the man, to whom every soldier looked for guidance and survival, was Sergeant Jake Tidwell, in his second tour of duty in Vietnam. Sergeant Tidwell had been in the battle for the A Shau Valley in 1969, and that fact alone evoked confidence in the man from every trooper and from the lieutenant, as well.

The jungle was, by its very nature, scary, even terrifying to some. There was danger around every turn and behind every tree. Frank preferred the daytime to the night. Night time brought new and different terrors. The stifling heat was only marginally more endurable at night. The frequent rain brought only a temporary respite that was soon replaced by a heavy steamy atmosphere that hung in the air for hours.

Manpower consisted of four sections, or squads of usually nine to eleven men each. Frank was assigned to first squad, which Sergeant Tidwell ordered to take a position on the left flank of the platoon. First squad's makeup included two *thumpers*, two soldiers carry M79 grenade launchers; a sergeant named Gronkowski, the squad leader; a Corporal Mendoza; an M60 team, operator and feeder; and one fire-team, four riflemen with M16s. Frank was a rifleman on the squad's small arms fireteam.

In the dim light of pre-dawn of the second day on station, Sergeant Tidwell spotted a detachment of NVA—North Vietnamese Army—coming toward their position. It appeared to be about twenty men, probing. When the enemy soldiers were close enough, Lieutenant Melton and Sergeant Tidwell ordered the troops to fire on them. The resulting action left many of the enemy troops dead and the rest withdrew, reformed, and attacked. A firefight ensued that lasted about twenty-five minutes. The platoon took no casualties and killed all the remaining enemy.

"They'll be more of them," Tidwell told his men, "They know we're here now. They'll be back."

The sergeant was right. After the probing attack of the previous day, additional elements of the 6th NVA Regiment attacked in force, and the men of second platoon fought for their lives. The jungle seemed to breed "little people" as they came from all directions.

The M60 teams did the bulk of the work in killing large numbers of the attacking enemy, but the riflemen fought the "dinks" close up, often hand to hand, once they had gotten into the perimeter. Men were yelling and cursing.

"Zips in the wire," screamed by terrified voices, was heard more than once as each soldier looked around frantically, to make sure the enemy had not gotten behind them. One man on Frank's fire team emptied his entire magazine into one enemy soldier who had broken through the M60's killing zone and invaded their position.

Sergeant Tidwell called in a fire support mission and artillery shells began landing in front of their line. The attack slowed a bit, but no one could relax because there were still enemy soldiers all around them. They were ordered to move into the jungle to scare up what was left of the attacking force. Small arms fire could be heard, on every side, as troops of second platoon would encounter remnants of the NVA soldiers and kill them. Frank and one of the men from his fire team came up on a wounded enemy soldier and both of them shot the man at the same time.

The engagement was not an untypical scenario. Frank's entire combat career in Vietnam had been one such engagement after another. He quickly came to believe that no one could do this kind of work, time and time again, and live through it. He vacillated between resignation that he was going to die in some jungle, somewhere and resolve to stay alive and go home to his wife and baby boy.

In May, Frank was scheduled for his first R & R. His father paid for airfare for Sarah and Frankie, now eight months old, to visit Frank in Hawaii.

It was like a dream for Sarah, who had never been out of Louisiana, a magic time in a magic place. They were ecstatically happy, the three of them. Frank adored his son, and made love to his wife, telling her of his love for her, and assuring her that his love would never end. Sarah was beautiful and garnered second looks from men everywhere they went."

"You're going to get me in a fight before this is over."

"I can't help it," she said, "I'm not even looking at anyone."

"You can't help being beautiful. I would have married an ugly woman if I didn't want men looking at my wife."

They visited Pearl Harbor. Frank wanted to see the battleship, *Arizona*, still lying on the bottom of the harbor, where it had gone down almost thirty-years before.

"It's almost unimaginable that over a thousand men are still down in that ship, right down there," he said, pointing at the sunken ship.

"It's just so sad," Sarah said, "such a terrible war and it didn't end anything. We're still fighting wars we have no business being in."

"I'll come back to you, darling, and this war will be over for us."

"I pray for you every day, Frank."

"Well, don't stop," he replied, "I need all the help I can get."

In November, Frank's tour was over and he returned to his wife and son. "I have to get a job, now," he said, "and a place for us to live."

Frank's father, Odell, implored them to stay with him, at least until Frank could get on his feet and afford to buy them a house. Sarah encouraged Frank to take his father's offer, and Frank conceded to her wishes. For Odell Ross, it was the happiest time of his life with his son, and his only grandson, living in the same house with him. And the touch of a woman, he'd grown accustomed to having around the house while Frank was away.

Frank got a job selling office equipment for a company in Baton Rouge. He began traveling all over the state, often staying overnight in motels, to be able to meet an appointment early in the mornings. He was good at his job and made a good living for his family.

Eventually, they were able to rent a house for their family and found a two-bedroom just down the street from Frank's father, on Janis Street. It was a small house but big enough for the three of them. "We'll buy a bigger house, as soon as we can," he told her.

But Sarah was content with what they had.

The owner of the house they were renting passed away, and his family wanted to sell the house. Not wanting to move and being unable to buy that bigger house at the time, Frank offered to buy the rented house from the man's family. The owners were eager to sell the house, so they consented. Frank went to the bank, secured a loan, and he and Sarah became homeowners.

"It's not much, baby, but it's ours," he told her.

"It's fine, Frank," she said, "and it's more than enough.

Frank wanted to have his own business, something that he and Sarah could own and manage, and that his son would one day take over when he was ready to retire. He had dreamed of building a bait and tackle supply facility on the river's edge. It would have boat launch ramps, boats to rent, crab traps and such, and sandwiches, drinks, and ice available for purchase.

Property, however, was very expensive on False River, but that did not deter his dreaming of such a business. The facility would have to be established in a more remote area, because Frank could never save enough money to buy waterfront property in town. Sarah got a part time job working for a CPA, answering the phone, filing, and helping with the bookkeeping. The job afforded her the time to take Frankie to school and pick him up in the afternoon.

Sarah was happy, happier than she ever imagined she could be. The lovable, over-confident, mildly abrasive boy, who had declared to her the first time they met that they were going to get married one day, had grown into a caring and wonderful husband and father.

"I put a thousand dollars into a mutual fund, Sarah. I'm going to add to it as I can. In case something happens to me, I took out a life insurance plan to help you and Frankie get by. It's only fifty grand but that would offset the loss of my income. You must leave the money in the mutual fund until you need it for retirement or in an extreme emergency."

"You're scaring me, Frank," she said, "you don't have a premonition, do you?"

"No, I just want to be prepared. I don't want you to have a struggle if something does happen to me."

"What exactly is a mutual fund?"

"It's a company that invests in stocks. We buy shares of the company and our shares go up or down, depending on how well the investments they make do in the market. Ours is a Fidelity fund. I've heard good things about Fidelity, so I think it's a safe investment. I can put two thousand a year in, tax deferred, like a retirement account, four thousand if we put in for you too."

"Okay," she said, "whatever you think is best, I trust your judgement. I don't know anything about investing."

"I'm also looking at some acreage along the river, it's far enough out of town that I think we might be able to buy it, if I can get financing."

"How much is it?"

"Property on the river is going to cost around fifty grand, minimum, but that's what we'll have to do to start the up the business."

"Wow, that's a lot of money, and the dock and building will more than double that, I'm guessing."

"We need a couple hundred thousand to just get started, honey. It's an uphill march, but if we are ever going to be anything but working stiffs, that's what we're looking at."

"I'm proud of you for what you're trying to do for us, Frank, and I'll help any way I can."

"You do help, Sarah," he told her, "just being here when I come home from work is all the help I need from you. You make me happy, baby."

"You make me happy, too, darling. My life has been pretty much perfect since I met you. You are so different from that boy who fed me a line of mush the first day of school, trying to get in my pants."

"It wasn't a line, Sarah, but to be honest, I did want in your pants pretty badly. I still do, and I still love you more and more every day."

"I still love you too," she told him, "and I appreciate what you do for us."

Two years passed before they were able to get a loan to purchase a two-acre plot of land on the river's edge. He took Sarah and Frankie to look at the land he'd bought.

They drove down False River Road, Route One, past the small community of Oscar to Cherie Lane. "It's just past Cherie Lane," he said, as he looked for a place to turn the car around. He pulled off the road and parked. "This is it, let's go take a look."

"I figure we'll use one acre for the parking lot, and turn-around. We'll have a gravel driveway and parking area, maybe have it paved one day. We'll put the building there," he said, pointing at the shoreline. "The dock will extend out past the sandbar, and we'll build boat shed at the end of it. I want to name it Riverbend Boat Rentals, for obvious reasons. It's right near the bend in the river."

"That makes sense to me, darling," Sarah said. "I'm really excited about it. I hope we can avoid getting too anxious to make this happen. It's going to cost a lot of money."

"We'll have to go slow," he said. "I know what you mean, though, I want to do it tomorrow, but I'll have to get control of my impatience."

"It's a beautiful place," Sarah said, "I can already picture it in my mind."

"Yeah, me too," he replied. "It's going to happen, baby, I promise you."

On the ride, back to town, a haunting thought came to Sarah. It was a warning from the bible she remembered from Sunday school. She looked it up when she got back home. It was in the book of Frank, coincidentally.

Come now, you who say, "Today or tomorrow we will go to this or that city, spend a year there, carry on business, and make a profit." You do not even know what will happen tomorrow! What is your life? You are a mist that appears for a little while and then vanishes.

Reading the passage, made Sarah fearful. "Are we moving too fast?" she asked Frank.

"What do you mean?"

She told him about the scripture she had remembered and was wondering if their ambition to better themselves might be sinful.

"I never paid much attention to the bible when I was growing up," he said. "I don't see anything wrong with a man trying to make life easier for his family."

"I think we should start going to church," Sarah said.

"I'm not much of a church person," he said, "you and Frankie are my church."

"But I believe that we should honor God and involve him in our plans and dreams. Don't you, darling?"

"I don't see God dropping two-hundred-grand in my lap, anytime soon. But I do see that we are going to have to work our asses off, if we ever hope to have anything in this world,"

Sarah let the subject drop, but she still had a fear, deep inside her, that kept nagging at her,

September 10, 1981 was Frankie Ross's twelfth birthday. Frank and Sarah had a party for him at False River Park, and several kids from his class showed up.

Adeline Connor, who was there with her father, Clay, handed Frankie a box with a ribbon on it. "I got this for you, Frankie," she said.

He quickly opened the box and found inside a brand-new baseball glove, which was obviously bought by her father.

"Wow, this is a great glove, Addy," Frankie said, "it's my favorite gift, thank you."

The girl insisted on sitting next to Frankie on the park bench when they ate their burgers and hot dogs that had been grilled by Frankie's dad. This birthday would be one that Frankie would never forget.

"The Connor girl seems to like Frankie," Frank said to Sarah, watching the two kids sitting together.

"She's a pretty little girl. I think Frankie kind of likes her too."

"He can fall in love with a pretty, rich girl, just as easy as he can with a mud-duck." Frank said.

"Now, that's just mean, Frank," she said, "ugly girls need love too." She laughed and smiled at him.

"And I don't begrudge them that love," he said, "as long as they don't want it from my boy."

"You're awful," she said and hit him lightly with the back of her hand, across his chest.

On the morning of January 14, 1981, Frank Ross woke up early, before dawn. He watched his wife, lying beside him, breathing rhythmically. He moved over next to her and put his arm around her, snuggling up to her neck and kissing it. Sarah woke up, turned toward him, and smiled. "What are you doing, darling?" she asked him.

"Let me love you, baby," he said quietly, "I need you."

He kissed her with almost desperate passion, and she responded with her own. He continued kissing her until she became aroused. She removed her pajamas and came to him in complete submission.

They made love for almost an hour, taking care to be quiet in the small house where their son was sleeping in the next room. "That was a pleasant surprise," she told him, when they had finished. "Why don't you do that more often?"

"You are incredible, baby," he said. "Nothing ever made me feel like you do."

"Kiss me some more."

He did as she had requested and kissed her again for a few minutes. "I have to go to work, Sarah," he said, "I have a long day today."

Sarah took Frankie to school and then went to her job at the CPA's office. After work, she retrieved Frankie from school, picked up a few items at the grocery store, and went home to start supper. It was seven o'clock and Frank had not come home from work. He said he had a long day, so Sarah was not worried.

When the phone rang, Sarah got a deep feeling of dread. "Hello," she said, and there was a pause. She suddenly felt like she had been hit with a rock, then she dropped the phone and fell to the floor.

"What's wrong, Momma?" Frankie yelled and ran to her. He shook her and picked her head up off the floor, weeping profusely, still shaking her, trying to wake her up.

Frank Ross's car had been blind-sided by a pickup truck being driven by a drunk driver. Sarah's husband, the love of her life and the father of her son, was dead at twenty-nine years of age.

☾☯☽

Sarah was suddenly aware that a man was standing behind her off to her left side. She stood up and took Frankie's hand. "Let's go, sweetie," she said, "these men need to put Daddy to rest."

She turned to go to her car and saw the man standing there. It was Clay Connor, a local businessman who lived in New Roads. He walked over to her and took her hand.

"I'm really sorry for your loss, Sarah," he told her, "Frank was a good man. I didn't think so at first, but after I got to know him, I came to realize that he was the right man for you. It almost broke my heart when you married him, but I watched him over the years, how he treated you and Frankie, and I know he loved you very much."

Clay was sincere, she could tell by his demeanor. Sarah knew that he had harbored a hurt and wounded pride and a broken heart, when she married Frank Ross. She knew that Clay was in love with her, at the time, but she had assumed he'd gotten over her.

He had gotten married, had three lovely daughters, and never paid her much attention after Frankie was born. On the occasional chance meetings they'd had, while Frank was in Vietnam, Clay had been courteous and respectful. She had not realized, until today, that Clay Connor had never stopped loving her.

In a small town, where everyone knew everyone else, a beautiful woman, left alone by the death of her husband, was a target for any unattached man who thought she might be an easy conquest. It was not long before men started hitting on her.

At first, she tried to respectfully decline their advances, but after a year had gone by, she became less diplomatic. "I don't date," she bluntly told a would-be suitor more than once.

One oaf approached her in the grocery store and put on his best redneck persona. "You gotta be gettin' horny by now," the man said, leering at her. "If I can be of any service to you, just give me a call."

"Piss off, you piece of shit," she told him, her voice dripping with vitriol. "If I ever do get horny, I sure as hell won't come to you for relief."

The man was visibly angry, at her chastising, but he had the good sense not to make a scene in public.

Another man, Tom Robillard, asked her to have dinner with him. He was respectful and considerate. "Sarah," he said, "we've known each other since elementary school. I've always known that you're a good woman. I'm really sorry about your husband, Frank. He was a good man. I liked him a lot, in school and after. I would love to take you out to dinner, no strings attached and no expectations. You're the prettiest woman in this town, and I just want to enjoy your company. If you don't want to be seen with me in New Roads, we can go to Baton Rouge where no one will know us.

Sarah was amused by his offer, and he did seem sincere. "Thank you, Tom," she told him, "I'm just not ready yet to start seeing someone. But if I were, I would not have a problem being seen with you in New Roads,"

"I understand," he said, "perhaps when you're ready, you'll consider my request again."

"September tenth, 1987," she said.

"What?"

"September 10, 1987, my son will be eighteen and, conceivably, on his own. Then I'll be ready."

"Oh, okay," he said, smiling broadly, "I'll mark my calendar, that's only four years away. If I am still above ground, on September 10, 1987, I'm going to ask you out to dinner. Thank you, Sarah."

"Thank you, Tom," she said, "you made me feel good."

Sarah paid off the house with the life insurance money from Frank's death. That left her forty-thousand dollars, of which she put half in the Fidelity Mutual Fund and kept the rest in the bank to make the payments on the land they had bought.

Frankie and the Connor girl were kind of an item. She could tell that her son was crazy about Addy Connor and, from what little she had seen of them together, the feelings appeared to be mutual.

What an interesting turn of events that would be, she was thinking, the daughter of the man who had loved her since high school marrying her son. It could happen, but no one could tell what might happen in the future. She had learned that lesson the hard way.

The CPA hired a full-time office manager, and Sarah's part-time job was no longer available to her. When she was in high school, she had worked as a waitress at Morels, a very popular restaurant on Main Street in New Roads. She had few other skills, so, after trying to find an office job and not being successful, she applied at Morel's and was hired.

It was hard work. A waitress was on her feet from the minute she clocked in until she walked out the door at quitting time. Her feet ached terribly. She soaked them in a small tub of water with Epsom salts every night. Frankie rubbed her feet for her and helped her more around the house. He cooked dinner on occasion and took her out to dinner when she didn't feel like eating at home.

"I feel terrible, sometimes, that I let you do so much around the house. You're too good to me, son," she often told him.

His response was always the same. "You're my mother. Helping you out every so often is the least I can do for all you've done for me. Mom, can I ask you a question?"

"Of course, dear," she said, "what's on your mind?

"Do you think you'll ever get married again?"

"I don't know, Frankie, maybe after you're grown up and are out on your own, I might. I don't think about it very much. Your dad was the love of my life. I know I'll never meet a man who measures up to him. But who knows? I might find me a man somewhere that I'll be able to tolerate."

He began chuckling, went over, and hugged her. "He'll be the luckiest guy in the world, if you ever do find him."

"Well, aren't you nice to me? Thank you, dear. That makes me feel like a shiny new dime."

"That's what Grandpa always says."

"I know. I hope you are spending time with him. He took the loss of your father very hard, and Grandpa's not in the best of health."

"I see him just about every day," Frankie said. "I help him clean up his house and walk to the store for him when he needs things.

"You are your father's son, Frankie."

"I miss him so much, Mom, I wish he hadn't died.

"I do too, dear, I miss him too," she said.

CHAPTER 2

The Connors

Clay Connor met Louise Whitley during their sophomore year in college. She was from money, her father being a financial wizard who had made his in the field of investment banking in New Orleans. Louise was a child of privilege who had been pampered with material things by absentee parents who had little time for her and her two older brothers.

She and Clay met at a mixer at the fraternity house of a friend of Clay's and began dating. Louise was an attractive woman but not much more than that. Clay found her easy enough to look at but did not consider her a beautiful woman. She was shapely and in possession of what

Clay referred to as lovely breasts, of which she was demonstrably proud.

"You keep staring at my breasts," she told him, the first time they met.

"I'm sorry," he said, visibly nervous. "You're very pretty, and I just can't help myself."

"It's okay," she said, "I take it as a compliment."

"Who are you?" he asked her.

"I'm me," she responded, coyly.

"No, I mean your name, what is your name?"

"Oh, yeah, I'm Louise Whitley and I'm from New Orleans. You've heard of New Orleans, haven't you?"

"Once or twice," he said, "I've even been there a couple of times. Whereabouts do you live in New Orleans?"

"My parents have a house on the Lakefront."

Clay just nodded. She had just told him that her folks were rich and that she had, most likely, come to college to find a rich husband. He was probably not going to be the man she was looking for. But he pursued her, nevertheless, his only interest in her, at the time, being to get her into bed.

"Do you have a name?" she asked him.

"I do," he responded, "if I can remember it."

She squealed with delight and started giggling.

"Oh, yeah, I remember now, it's Clayton, Clayton Connor, but I go by Clay."

Despite her Catholic upbringing, Louise was not a difficult conquest for Clay. He took her to his off-campus apartment on the pretext of cooking her dinner, which he did, and then taking her to bed, which he also did. Eventually, he revised the scenario, in his mind, to reflect her eager participation in the activities of that night. They began sleeping together on a regular basis, and soon she had moved all her clothes and things, out of her dorm room into his apartment. She told Clay that she was in love with him. It caught him by surprise and, although flattering, changed his life and scared the hell out of him.

Louise was a woman with little subtlety and left nothing to the imagination. "You love me too, don't you, Clay?" she asked him, almost frantically.

"I don't know, Louise," he said, flustered. "I enjoy being with you, but I haven't thought about that yet. We barely know each other."

"I'm pregnant," she told him, "You'd better start thinking about it."

"You're pregnant, Louise?" he said. "You're not on the pill?"

"Of course, I'm not on the pill, my family is Catholic. We don't believe in using birth control."

"You don't believe in sex before marriage, either," he said, "but that didn't stop you from jumping into bed with me. If you can break one rule, why can't you break another one?"

"I don't know. What are we going to do, Clay?"

"How far along are you?"

"About two months, as far as I can tell. I haven't been to a doctor yet, I've missed my period."

"Then you don't know for sure," he said. "Wait until you see a doctor and then we'll decide what to do. This is all I need," he said to himself, out loud.

Clay was still nursing a broken heart from losing the girl he loved to another man. He had planned to ask Sarah Mayeux to marry him when she graduated from high school. He would have been on his way to earning a business degree and able to offer her a comfortable and relatively worry-free life with him. They would have children and be happy. But Sarah fell in love with an up-start, a stranger, who came into her life suddenly and un-expectedly. She had become pregnant, and they were married and, just like that, she was out of his life forever.

He could not envision spending the rest of his life with Louise Whitley. But he also could not fathom walk-ing away from a child he had fathered. He decided to go talk to his father at his main office in Baton Rouge.

Clay Connor Senior had built his business from the ground up. Connor Enterprises was a company that owned other companies. Clay's parents had moved from New Roads to Baton Rouge when their son started to school at LSU. The senior Connor intended for his son to take over the business when he got his business degree. Clay Junior had been willing and eager to do that very thing until his unrequited love for Sarah ruined his life and threw him into a depression that he sometimes believed would never go away.

"I may have to get married, Pop," he told his dad when he met him at the office.

"You knock up some gal?" Mister Connor said.

"I don't know, maybe, I don't know yet,"

"Well, hell, son, it's not the end of the world. Do you love her?"

"I barely know her, Pop, she says she loves me."

"You better figure out if you can live with her or not. You must think of your child first. Are you sure it's yours?" Clay nodded.

"It's mine, I'm sure of that," he said.

"Well, you have to marry someone eventually. Just don't forget your first priority. You have to stay in school until you get that degree."

"I may have to go to work to support them," he said.

"We can work that out. You can help me out, maybe part-time, until you finish school. What's the girl's name?"

"Louise," Clay said.

"Kind of a shitty name," the elder Connor said, grimacing.

"I know," Clay, replied, "but she's got nice tits."

His father smiled and gave him a thumb up.

Louise turned out to be as fertile as the Rio Grande Valley and was indeed with child. The Whitleys, Louise's parents, didn't want to have a big wedding for their daughter, for fear that their friends would know that Louise had been impregnated by a man she had slept with at college. That revelation would not have supported the narrative that Oliver and Mona Whitley had endeavored to cultivate to the good people and priests at St Monica's Catholic Church in New Orleans. So, Clay and Louise were married in Baton Rouge, in a small ceremony at the home of Clay's parents.

Louise quit school to take care of the baby, a girl, born in August of 1968. They named the girl Marie Louise. Clay was ecstatic and proud to have a daughter. She was, in his mind, sufficient reward from the almighty for having to endure the constant prattling and complaining of his wife, Louise. Another daughter came along in September of the following year. They named her Cathryn, with no middle name. The apartment was getting smaller very quickly.

"I can't keep living off your money, Dad," Clay told his father. "I have to make a living for my family."

"I don't want you to drop out of school, son, that will mess up our plans."

"I need to go to work full time, and I need a bigger place to live. The apartment is too small with two babies."

"Okay, listen to me," his father said. "I've been having the house in New Roads remodeled, so I can sell it. Why don't you move your family into the house and you can keep the apartment, or move into a dorm room, until you finish your degree. You only have one year left, don't blow it now."

Clay nodded. "That sounds good. Let me talk to Louise about it."

"Do you think Louise will be happy in a small town like New Roads?" Clay senior asked him.

"I don't think Louise is going to be happy anywhere, Dad, to be honest."

Louise was adamant about not wanting to be relegated to a town of less than five-thousand people, until she saw the house. "It's beautiful, Clay," she said, "I love it."

He was surprised, yet pleased, and thankful. It was one less thing for them to fight about.

In August, of 1969, Hurricane Camille hit the Gulf Coast, smashing into the Mississippi coast on the night of August seventeenth, and left a path of destruction until the early hours of August eighteenth.

It was several days before Louise was able to make contact with her parents. East New Orleans received a tremendous amount of damage and the lakefront was torn up badly.

The Whitleys, however, were okay. They had gotten out early, across the Lake Pontchartrain Causeway through Mandeville, and north to Franklinton, where they waited it out.

Finally, reaching her father at his office, she was relieved to hear his voice and find them still alive and well.

"I can come there and help you, if you need me to, Daddy," Louise told him.

"No, no," he replied, "you won't be able to get in,
there's too much going on right now. I'll keep you informed. I'm going out to the house later today to inspect
the damages."

After learning that her parents were okay, and with
the move into the new house, Louise was happy for a
time. In early March of 1970, she discovered that she was
pregnant, again. "A boy this time, please, ma'am," Clay
petitioned her, but it was not to be. A baby girl came on
October third. Clay was philosophical about it. "I knew it
would be one or the other."

They named the girl Adeline Victoria and she was
beautiful.

"You're going to have to get on the pill, Louise."
Clay told her. "We simply can't afford to have a baby
every time we get together."

"I'll go on the pill, Clay," she finally conceded.

Clay graduated in May of 1971 and moved into the
house in New Roads permanently. The commute to the
office was just over forty miles into Baton Rouge but
didn't take as long as some folks had to contend with in
bigger cities, like New Orleans. Traffic was always light
in and out of New Roads and didn't start to slow down
until he hit the freeway, headed into Baton Rouge.

Clay was able to get a home mortgage loan and
bought the house from his dad. The residence seemed

much nicer and, somehow more permanent, when the title was in his name. He had a dock and boat house built at the river's edge. A twenty-six-foot Catalina, Bowrider, took the family out on the lake almost every weekend while the girls were growing up. Often, Clay would take the boat out by himself and spend the day doing nothing. He was not a fisherman, and Louise always questioned him about his time on the water, alone.

A small town, anywhere in the world, was but a microcosm of the world at large. New Roads was no different from every small town in the country, and in the world, for that matter. There was a caste system in play. The well-off residents, an exclusive group to which the Connor family belonged, gravitated toward each other's company. The less well-off typically stayed in their place and rarely penetrated the unspoken barrier that separated them. They mowed the yards, painted the houses, and performed any number of sundry tasks for those who could afford to pay them to do things they were either unable, or unwilling, to do for themselves.

Louise Connor joined the women's club and several other social entities that met frequently to organize charitable events and other functions, the intentions of which were to benefit the town and/or the less fortunate. In truth, they were not much more than gossip-fests and opportunities for back-biting and critical examination of this person or that one, most often being the person who was not in attendance at the time.

It was through this venue that Louise learned of her husband's former love interest, Sarah Mayeux.

"Oh, they were quite an item at one time, in New Roads," Eve Cormier (Corm-yay) informed her, on numerous occasions. "Your husband was considered quite a catch. He's a handsome man, I don't mind telling you, Louise."

"I thought so, too, when I first met him. So, who is this woman you're talking about?" Louise replied.

"She's a local woman. Sarah and Clay met at church. She was two years younger than him and was a very flighty girl. I think she led him on, if you want to know what I think. They dated regularly when he came home on weekends from LSU."

"What happened to her, Eve?" Louise asked.

"Oh, she's still around, lives over on Janis Street, not far from your house. You'd better keep an eye on that woman."

"No, I mean what happened to her that kept Clay from marrying her?"

"Oh, that," Eve said "Last year of high school, Sarah met a boy and got knocked up. They got married but he was killed in a car wreck in 1981. She never remarried, so you better keep an eye on her."

Louise was fuming as she drove home from Eve's house. "That bitch was enjoying telling about Clay's former love affair," she said out loud, with venom. She seethed about it for a week or so and then could contain herself no longer. "Tell me about Sarah, Clay," she demanded, one evening at dinner.

"There's nothing to tell, Louise," he said. "We dated for a while when we were younger. She married Frank Ross and had a son. Frankie is about the same age as Adeline, he's a good boy. There is nothing else to tell."

"That's not what I hear," she said.

"Don't believe everything you hear at those hen parties, Louise."

"I don't, but if you still have feelings for this woman, that's not fair to me and the girls."

"I don't, Louise," he said. "Put it out of your mind. You'll get yourself all worked up over nothing."

When Adeline was eleven-years-old, she asked her dad to take her to the birthday party of a friend from school.

"Did he give you a card or something telling you when and where it will be?" Clay asked her.

She handed him the invitation card. The party would be at False River Park on September tenth. The boy's name was Frankie Ross. Clay immediately recognized the possible repercussions of taking his daughter to that event. Nevertheless, he decided he would do it. He took her to buy a gift, a baseball glove, because, as his daughter explained to him, "Frankie likes baseball."

His wife did not make the connection. She didn't actually know Frankie Ross. She might have heard his name at one of her "socials." But Louise was a self-absorbed woman and, unless someone told her specifically who Frankie Ross was, it was unlikely that she would even have given it a second thought.

At the park, the kids were playing. There were about ten or twelve of them. Clay sat at the picnic table close to where Frankie's dad was grilling burgers and hot dogs. Sarah Ross came over and sat down across the table from him. Frank Ross brought him a burger and took condiments, lettuce, tomatoes, and such out of the ice chest, "Eat all you want, Clay," Frank said, "There's plenty more.

"I'm good, Frank," Clay said. "This will be enough for me, thanks."

Sarah was watching the kids playing. "Addy is a beautiful girl, Clay, and Frankie says she is very smart. You must be very proud of her."

"I'm proud of all my girls, Sarah, I didn't deserve such good children."

"Frankie is very fond of Addy. He talks about her all the time."

"That's a little ironic, isn't it?" Clay said.

Sarah smiled. "He's a good boy, Clay."

"I know he is, I can tell by watching him interact with Adeline. I'd like to take him out on the boat with us sometime, if you don't mind."

"I think that would be nice," she said.

And so began Clay Connor's long-term relationship with the son of his lost love. He discovered that Frankie was indeed a fine young man, respectful and considerate, and not afraid of work. After an afternoon on the river, with his daughters and a couple of friends, and Frankie Ross, Frankie was the only one who would hang around and help Clay clean the boat and sack up the trash. He taught Frankie how to drive and handle the boat when Frankie was fifteen. His daughter's affection for the boy was not lost on anyone, especially Louise Connor.

"Who is this boy you say you like?" she asked her daughter.

"Frankie," Addy said, "Frankie Ross, he goes to my school."

"What about his family, Adeline, what do they do and where do they live?"

"Frankie's daddy is dead. He was killed in a car wreck when Frankie was twelve. He lives with his mother, on Janis Street," Addy said.

Louise was waiting for Clay when he came home from the office that afternoon. "What the hell are you trying to pull on me, Clay Connor?" she screeched at him. After telling him about her conversation with their youngest daughter, she demanded answers.

"Adeline likes the boy, Louise, she likes him a lot. I'm not going to shun him just because of who he happens to be and who his mother is."

"I don't want Adeline seeing that boy, anymore."

"That is not your decision to make," he said.

The complaining continued, but Louise was not a

strong-willed person, despite being a serial nagger. She never agreed, but eventually stopped her griping because her husband was stoic and resolute when he made up his mind about something.

Louise had discovered, in the years since they had been married, that the best way to persuade her husband to see things her way was with sweetness, submission, and conciliation. Manipulation and calculating were Louise's best weapons.

"Why have you been avoiding, me, Clay?" she would often ask him at night, after they were in bed.

"If I've been doing that, I'm sorry, I've been tired lately. My workload has been almost overwhelming."

"Will you make love to me?"

He would look at her, an almost pleading look on her face. The truth was that he was attracted to his wife. She was a good-looking woman, not drop-dead gorgeous, as the saying went, but good looking. Their love life had not been the detriment to their having a happy marriage. It was the only positive, besides his daughters, that kept him with her, in any kind of mutually satisfying relationship. She was good in bed, very vocal and complimentary of his abilities. He wished that their compatibility in the bedroom would carry over to the rest of their life together.

Frankie Ross continued to come to the house with Addy, and Clay let him take the boat out on the river anytime the two kids asked him.

Eventually, Clay's father retired from the business, and Clay took over as CEO. His salary and bonuses, as well as other benefits increased exponentially. The Connors became rich, richer being a more accurate assessment of their financial situation, and Louise wanted to move out of New Roads, either to Baton Rouge or New Orleans.

Clay would not even discuss it with her. "I'm not leaving our house, Louise," he told her. "I'll rent a small apartment in Baton Rouge, for nights when I work late and don't feel like driving home. You can come with me, and we'll spend a weekend, go out to dinner, or to see your folks. I'll do everything I can to make you happy, but I'm not moving out of New Roads."

He ended up buying a condominium, in which he began staying one or two nights a week. The drive from Baton Rouge to his house was not his primary reason for staying overnight in the condo. He enjoyed the time away from his wife. With two of the three girls gone, only Adeline and the two of them remained in the big house on False River. Clay's life became a lonely place to live. Adeline would leave to attend LSU, a year later, then it would become almost unbearable for him.

CHAPTER 3

The Summer of '88

With the approach of summer, the senior graduates of Rosenwald High School were in expectant anticipation of three months of fun and water sports.

One graduate in particular, Addy Connor would be starting at LSU in the fall. And she was insistent that Frankie Ross spend his summer with her on the river or engaged in other means of frivolity before she entered an institution of higher learning and was forced to accept the seriousness of her life and its future.

But Frankie had a full-time job, a job he had worked since he had graduated the year before Addy.

Driving around the lake was one of Addy's favorite things. She and Frankie made the trip quite frequently. It was like an afternoon "mini-date" for the two them

Addy drove, and Frankie looked at her. She was only five foot, three inches, so she had to pull the seat of her car up to and almost right under the steering wheel. Main Street in New Roads turned into highway 413 at the edge of town and circumvented the lake.

There were numerous secluded areas on the other side, into which they could pull the car off the road and not be seen by passersby.

The two lovers, locked in each other's embrace, would engage in a half-hour of power kissing until Addy decided that it was time to stop.

"I'm working for Mister Mike full time now so that means this summer," he told her, as they were headed back to town. "I have to help my mother with the bills."

"I know," she said, "but we can do things after you get off work. I just don't want to waste the summer."

"I'm off on the weekends. There'll be plenty of time for us."

"I want to go out on Daddy's speedboat, and you're the only one he lets drive it besides him. He says you're the most responsible friend I have."

"That's because I don't drink, like all your other friends."

"But I don't drink," she said.

"You can't drink, you're only seventeen. You'll be

able to drink on your next birthday, which is about five months from now, but I hope you don't."

"I won't," she said.

"Good, promise me that and I'll take off a day, every so often, and take you out in the boat."

"I promise," she said.

"You're going to be under a lot of pressure when you start college. A lot of kids go to college to party. I hope you stay focused on our plan."

"I will," she said, "what was our plan again?"

"You're toying with me," he said, shaking his head.

"You're just always so serious, Frankie, you need to lighten up and have some fun."

"You're my only fun, Addy, I love you. I don't need anything else."

"I love you too," she said, "but we don't have to be so serious all the time."

"I'm sorry, Addy, it's just different with me. My folks were never well-off. My dad was a good man, and he worked hard to support us, but he was killed by a drunk driver. He was doing everything right, coming home from work to be with his family, and he was broad-sided by a drunk driver. It wasn't his fault, and it wasn't fair, but that's what happened."

"I'm really sorry, Frankie," Addy said, "I wish things were different."

"My mom works harder than she should have to, and I have to help her." He looked at her, lovingly. "You're so beautiful, Addy, I'm afraid I'll lose you when you go away to college."

Her brown hair, kept cropped to a couple of inches below her chin, shimmered in the sunlight, and her big brown eyes, so brown they almost looked black, smiled at him. She reached up and pushed the left side of her hair behind her ear. She typically wore it that way. It exposed more of her face, and Frankie liked her hair that way.

"If you'll tuck both sides of your hair behind your ears, I can see more of your pretty face," he told her."

"It makes me look goony like that."

"No, it doesn't," he said. "You're the prettiest girl in town, nothing makes you look goony."

"It's a small town," she said.

"Do I have to convince you, once again, that you're beautiful? I think you just like hearing me say it."

"I do like hearing you say it, you say it so well."

"I'll tell you every day for the rest of our lives when we get married."

"My daddy wants me to finish college before we get married."

"I know," he replied, "and I'm okay with that."

Mister Mike was Mike Gaudin—pronounced Go-Dan—who owned an electrical contracting company in New Roads. Mike contracted commercial and residential projects and service work, all over Pointe Coupee Parish. Frankie had gone to work for Gaudin in the summer between his freshman and junior years in school and often worked on Saturday when the boss needed him.

It is a common proclivity, throughout the South, and more specifically in Louisiana, for younger people to address their elders by Mister, or Miss, and then add their first names. It is an expression of both respect and familiarity. Mister Mike Gaudin had taken Frankie under his wing, as the saying goes, and was teaching him to be an electrician.

Frankie Ross was Mike's most reliable employee. The young man was always on time, did not miss work, and could always be counted on to work Saturdays, if he was needed. Mike let him drive one of the service trucks home every day, after work, so he would have transportation back and forth to the shop.

"Take Tuco and Eddie, load up boxes and wire for a two-bedroom in the new project in St. Francisville." Mike gave instructions, and the address, to Frankie. He gave him cash for the ferry and sent them on their way. Frankie drove to the St. Francisville ferry landing and they waited for the boat to arrive.

After crossing the Mississippi, they drove to the St. Francisville housing project and found the jobsite. Frankie marked the box locations and laid out the house for Eddie and Tuco.

The two helpers began nailing up the switch and receptacle boxes, while Frankie drilled holes for the cables to run through.

They broke for lunch around eleven. Each man had brought sandwiches and drinks which were iced down in the cooler. Tuco finished his lunch very quickly, leaned back against a stud in the wall, and fell asleep. At eleven-thirty, Frankie woke him up. "Time to get back to work, guys," he told them, and they picked up where they had left off. By two o'clock the wiring was all done, and Frankie started making up the electrical panel. "Start making up the switches and plugs, Eddie," he said, "Tuco, can you build the service?"

"Sure, Frankie," he said, "I'll get right on it, as soon as I take a leak."

Making up meant to strip the outer sheath off the cable assembly, which is known as Romex. Then exposing the individual, insulated conductors, *pig-tailing* the wires and making them ready to attach to a receptacle or switch. The electrical panel cables had to be stripped and the neutrals and grounding conductors landed on terminal bars. The current carrying conductors are rolled up and left in the panel, to be connected to circuit breakers, at a later date, when they did the *trim-out*. By four o'clock, they were finished with the house. Frankie did the paperwork, so the next crew would know what material to bring for the finish out. They then drove back to the ferry landing and waited for the ferry to take them back across the river to New Roads.

Frankie walked from his house on Janis Street to the Connor's on Main. Clay Connor came to the door. "Hey,

Frankie," he said, "Adeline is waiting for you on the dock, you want to come in?"

"I can walk around, Mister Connor," Frankie replied.

"Okay, I'll be out in just a few minutes."

Frankie found her next to the boat, she had her bathing suit on but was wearing sweat pants. "Hey, beautiful," he said, "how are you?"

"I'm okay now. I've been waiting for you."

"Sorry, Addy, I had some chores to run for my mom this morning."

"Let's get going," she said, "my sisters are coming in for the weekend, and I don't want them to go with us."

"Your dad said he'd be out in just a few minutes."

"Yeah, he had the thingamabobs, that steer the boat, adjusted and he wants to tell you about it."

"That would be the steering cables, sweet-cheeks, not thingamabobs," he said.

In a few minutes, Clay Connor, came out to the dock. "The boat was getting a little slack in the steering, Frankie, so I had them tightened up. Just check it out and, if they're still acting up, come on back in."

"Yes, sir, Mister Connor, I'll be careful."

"I know you will, thanks, Frankie."

The boat was a twenty-six-foot Bowrider with two outboard engines. Frankie didn't know how fast it would go because he'd never opened it up. He was like an old man, Addy told him, but he remained overly cautious. An accident or even superficial damage to the boat, caused by reckless operation, might negatively affect the confidence Addy's father had in him, and he was not going to risk that.

He ran up and down the lake, for a half hour or so, to check the steering and found it working properly. Then he took it in to about two-hundred feet from shore and cut the engines. "I'll drop the anchor so, if we fall asleep, we won't drift into something, or somebody."

Addy removed her sweat pants and Frankie took off his clothes and climbed into the bow seating area with Addy. They immediately began kissing, which was not uncommon for them. It happened every time they got together. Addy never let it go too far, and after some time, she pulled away from him. "I'm starting to enjoy this a little too much," she told him.

"I reached that point, with the first kiss," he said.

"I could tell," she said, "guys have a way of letting a girl know."

He chuckled. "I'm sorry, Addy, I'm not rushing you. I just can't help it."

"I want to do it with you, before I leave for college," she said.

Frankie swallowed hard and he almost started hyperventilating. "You do?" he said.

"If you want to," she replied.

"I want to, Addy, you know I want to." He kissed her again and then leaned back against the seat. Just knowing it was going to happen made him feel like a shiny new dime, as his grandpa, Odell, used to say.

Addy put her feet in his lap and began tickling his stomach with her toes. He took her left foot in his hand and started caressing it, softly. He took her big toe between his thumb and index finger. "This little piggy went to market," he began to recite. "this little piggy stayed home."

When he got to the little piggy that stayed home, he took her pinky toe in his fingers and rubbed it gently. He touched a spot on the underside of her pinkie toe, and she let out a whoop, loudly, and started giggling.

"What was that?" he asked her, astonished at what she had done.

"It's a quirk," she said, "I've had it since I was a baby. My daddy found it when he was bathing me the first time. He was washing my feet and rubbed my pinkie toe and I squealed and started giggling. It does it every time."

"What causes that?"

"I don't know," she said, "some kind of neurological disorder, I suppose. Daddy used to drive me crazy doing it."

"So, you do have a flaw," he said, "I was wondering how one girl could be so perfect." He grabbed her foot and rubbed the toe again, and, just as before, she whooped and began giggling. "Stop," she said, "stop, I can't stand it."

He stopped and shook his head. "You're weird," he said.

When they got back to the Connor boat dock, Frankie maneuvered the boat into its slip and secured it. "Let's pick up our soft-drink cans and candy wrappers," he told her, and she began helping him put the stuff in the trash can.

"Daddy really likes you because you respect his property. Most of my other friends would just leave the boat tied up at the dock and wouldn't help him clean up anything."

"That's just not right. Your dad lets me use his boat to take his beautiful daughter out on the lake. The least I can do is leave them both in good condition."

"I love you, Frankie," she said, almost as if she were trying to convince herself of her feelings for him.

"I love you too, Addy," he replied, "I hope you mean that."

"Do I have to prove it to you?"

"No, you don't, you said you wanted to do it before you leave for college. I won't hold you to it, if you really want to wait until we are married."

"I don't want to wait, but where can we go? It's too risky at my house, and there is always someone there."

"You want to do it now?" he said, as he felt his heartbeat accelerate, dramatically.

"If you do," she said.

"My mother is working, there's no one at my house."

In his room, he kissed her. He was noticeably nerv-ous and could barely catch his breath.

"I'm scared, Frankie," she said, "I've never done this before."

"Neither have I, Addy," he told her, "but I love you, I really love you."

"I love you too, Frankie.

It was an awkward and a clumsy encounter, for the both of them. But millions, even billions of people, had been in the very same situation as the two teenagers now found themselves. And all those people figured it out and had gotten through it.

When they had finished, they lie there, in his bed, smiling at each other. "I had a lot of things I planned to say, when this happened, but I can't remember any of them right now," he said.

"It's okay, Frankie, you don't have to say anything. I liked it, I really liked it, I'm glad we did it."

By the end of July, they had become more proficient in the art of making love. They marveled at how easy it became, the more often they did it. The nervousness was gone, and they no longer hesitated to take their clothes off in front of each other. Frankie Ross could hardly con-tain himself. He and Addy begin to act differently in pub-lic. They would touch each other more frequently, and his arm was almost always around her shoulders. They kissed in front of her parents. They were too young to realize that two young people who are in an intimate relationship cannot hide it from the prying eyes of adults. It became obvious to Frankie's mother, Sarah, and also to Addy's parents.

It was Louise Connor, Addy's mother, who had the impertinence to confront her daughter about it. "Are you having sex with Frankie Ross?" she asked one evening at the dinner table.

Addy's first inclination was to lie, but her demeanor answered her mother's question before Addy could think of a response.

"You are, aren't you?" she wailed. "Clay, this is your doing, you've always treated that boy like he's your son. Now, he's screwing your daughter."

Addy screamed back at her, "It's not like that, Momma, I love Frankie."

"You're too young to know what love is," she threw back at her.

"No, I'm not," she yelled, "Daddy, make her stop."

"Now, Louise, calm down. It's not the end of the world."

"Do you want her marrying that boy?" she spewed at him.

"Actually, Louise, I'd be proud for my daughter to marry Frankie Ross. He's a fine boy."

"I'm not surprised, I should be, but I'm not. You're still in love with that whore, aren't you?"

"Shut up, Louise," he shouted and stood up. Addy had never seen her father so angry.

"What are you going to do, hit me? You know it's true, you never got over her,"

"I told you to shut up, Louise. Addy, please go to your room."

"What's she talking about, Daddy, who does she mean?"

Clay looked at Addy, almost pleadingly, "Please go to your room, baby," he said.

Addy got up, left the table, and went to her room. She was still crying, when her dad knocked on the door, a short while later. "Come on in, Daddy," she said.

He sat down on her desk chair, and she was sitting on the side of her bed. "I'm sorry about your mother, honey, but she does have a legitimate concern. Don't get me wrong, Adeline, I'm a little disappointed that you would be intimate with a boy at your young age. I guess, if it had to happen, I'm happy that it was with Frankie because I know you care for him and any fool can see that he is in love with you. But my concern, and your mother's as well, is that you could get pregnant. If you get pregnant now, it would ruin your plans to go to college and force you into an earlier marriage than you have been planning."

"I'm not going to tell you that I'm sorry for making love with Frankie, but I am sorry for disappointing you, Daddy."

"I said I was a little disappointed, honey, I'm not mad at you. I understand how things can happen between people and go too far. I just think you should be careful."

"Who was Momma talking about, Daddy?" she asked him.

"Something that happened a long time ago, honey, it doesn't concern you."

"She was talking about Frankie's mother, wasn't she?"

"That was a long time ago," he said, "I got over it, but your mother has never believed me."

Addy went to bed that night, thinking about Sarah Ross. Frankie's mother was a beautiful woman and it had been six years since Frank Ross died. She never saw Sarah so much as look at a man since she lost her husband. The woman never dated, not even dinner out, or at any of the local events, crawfish boils, parades, she never seemed to express any interest in finding another husband, or even just a boyfriend.

Had her father once been in love with Frankie's mother, maybe before Frankie was born, and before Sarah married Frankie's father? She guessed it was possible, her mother apparently believed it. But Louise Connor was generally thought to be partially unstable by her husband and friends and her three daughters as well.

Addy considered, for a moment, that her father might be Frankie's father too. That thought repulsed her, because that would make Frankie her brother, and that was too terrible to contemplate, so she didn't contemplate it. Frankie didn't look like Clay Connor, and he did look like the man in the pictures Frankie showed her of his dad. So, she buried that possibility.

Addy's parents had been fighting for as long as she could remember. Her sisters, Marie and Cathryn, went to college just to get away from the constant bickering of their mother. Their father, Clay, never seemed to lose his temper and, on the rare occasions when he did, he would leave the house and walk down Main Street into town. There he would sit in a booth in the local diner and drink coffee for an hour or longer, until he figured his wife had calmed down. Then he would walk back home. At other times, he would take his boat out on the lake and contemplate the futility of his life.

In Late August, Addy packed her things in her car and left New Roads, and Frankie Ross, for her new life at LSU in Baton Rouge. It was only forty miles from New Roads, but it would be a different world for Addy. She didn't know what to expect but with confidence, expectation, and a bit of trepidation, she embarked on a new chapter in her life.

Clay Connor was now alone, or at least he was alone with his wife. His three girls were gone now, and in all likelihood, would never live under his roof again. He was saddened by that but accepted it for what it was, the natural flow of human life. Birds leave the nest and children leave their parents to seek and build their own lives. Clay's reason for staying with Louise Connor all these years was gone. He had come to grips with the fact that he did not want to go on living like he'd been living for the last twenty years. He wanted another life and, most of all he wanted another woman. He wanted a woman who was still in love with her dead husband, and, most likely, would never love him.

CHAPTER 4

Addy

Clay had thought about asking his daughter, Adeline, to live in the Condo while she was going to LSU. Then he realized that he was being selfish, wanting to hold on to her for just a while longer, and he decided against it. Addy wanted to stay in the dormitory, meet new friends, and find out what life was really all about.

The first day of check-in, Addy found her room and put her things away. Her roommate did not arrive until the next morning.

She heard a key being inserted into the lock on her door and saw the knob turning. A blonde-haired girl, a little taller than Addy, entered the room with both hands clutching suitcases and other bags. Addy rushed over to help her with her belongings.

"Thank you," the girl said.

"Do you have more stuff to bring up?"

"I can get that later," she said, "I'm Cherry Pendergrass."

"I'm Adeline Connor, but I go by Addy.

"Where are you from, Addy?"

"I'm from a very small town called New Roads. It's about forty miles northwest of here," Addy told her. "Where are you from?"

"My family lives in Alexandria now, but I was born in Colorado. My parents are from there originally. Have you ever been to Colorado?"

"I've never been anywhere," Addy said. "My two older sisters married men they met in college and have been all over the country. I've been to New Orleans, my mother's parents live there, but I don't see them very often. Baton Rouge and New Roads are pretty much my only haunts, so to speak.

"So, what's your plan for college, you here to find a husband, like your sisters did?" Cherry asked her.

"No, I want to teach school," Addy replied. "I already have a husband—he's not my husband yet, but we plan to get married after I graduate."

"This is a guy at home?"

"Yes, Frankie Ross is his name, we've been boyfriend and girlfriend since we were twelve years old."

"Have you done it with him?"

"Yes," Addy said, "he's the only guy I've ever been with."

"You need to shop around, girl. Don't make a decision to marry the only guy you've ever been to bed with until you experiment. You might find someone better, maybe an upperclassman whose family has money."

Addy had never heard anyone talk like Cherry did. But, despite her initial shock of hearing her roommate's somewhat cynical outlook on life, she grew to like the girl. Cherry was worldly and seemed to Addy to have a good understanding of how the world worked.

She told her dad about Cherry at their next dinner out. She left out the part about the girl's suggestion that Addy sleep around a bit before she married her lifelong boyfriend.

"Thank you for taking me to dinner, Daddy," she told him. "I hope we can continue, but my schedule is going to be full, and I may be able to do it only a couple times a month."

"I suppose I can settle for taking you to dinner a couple of times a month, when you can find the time," her dad told her.

She was concerned that she might have hurt his feelings, and she wanted to correct herself. "I'll make time, anytime you want to take me to dinner, Daddy," she responded.

But as the school year played out, she was always busy, and their time together grew more infrequent. Addy had a room in Blake Hall. The dorm seemed to be bustling with activity, all the time, with a lot of things going on at night. It was exciting, a little intimidating, but she looked forward to being on her own. She was somewhat less on her own, with her father working in Baton Rouge, but Clay Connor had always trusted his girls to do the right thing and he gave them a fairly long leash.

Adeline was always his favorite, being the youngest and the one who turned out to be the Daddy's girl of the three. He was their rock, a calm port in a storm, and the only parent the girls could go to for advice and guidance when they were contending with their mother.

"Call your mother," he told her on numerous occasions, "she's bugging me about it. She says you're never in your room, when she calls."

"I'm sorry, Daddy, I'll call her, I promise."

"I hope you do, honey, she's not going to stop pushing me until you call her."

"But she calls every day, I just don't have time to spend an hour on the phone every morning."

"I understand," he said, "but if you can come home every other weekend or so, it would help to calm her down."

Addy went home for the weekend, made the obligatory visit with her mother, and then called Frankie. She asked her dad about using the boat, and as long as Frankie would be there, he consented.

"I want to do it in the boat," she told Frankie.

"Do what?" he asked.

"Make love, silly, what did you think I meant?"

"I wanted to hear you say it."

"You're okay with it, aren't you?" she said.

"Yes, Addy, I'm okay with it."

Had either of them been taller people, making love in the bow of the boat would have been challenging. But Frankie Ross was five feet, nine inches tall and Addy was only five-three. He spread a blanket over them and they both took off their swim suits and came together in a lover's embrace. It was no longer awkward for them, having made love only with each other for the past summer and during Addy's previous visits home. They were like a married couple, Frankie thought, no longer shy, or otherwise restrained.

"That was wonderful, Frankie," she said, as he was trying to catch his breath. "I needed that, you've spoiled me."

"I missed you, Addy," he said. "I dream about you every night."

"I'm going to come home every other weekend," she said.

"I hope you do, this town is mighty lonely without you here."

Addy and Cherry became good friends, despite their

differences, and decided to be roommates in their sopho-more year. After the summer of 1989 ended much too quickly for Frankie and Addy, she began her second year in college in September.

There were things to do in Baton Rouge on Saturday night, however, and before long, Addy was skipping her weekends going home. Her roommate, Cherry, made friends easily and began devoting more time to partying than she was to her studies. "I met a guy," she told Addy, "he's a junior and a stone fox, you have to meet him."

"I have to go home this weekend, I promised Frankie."

"Next weekend, then," Cherry said. "Rob has a roommate I want you to meet."

"I don't want to meet a guy. I'm in a relationship. You know that."

"It's just for dinner, no strings, I promise. I told Rob how pretty you are, and he wants his roommate, Jerry, to meet you."

"I'm not going to cheat on my boyfriend, Cherry," Addy insisted.

"It's not cheating," Cherry said, "they just want to take us out to dinner. We can go in separate cars, so you won't have to do the obligatory good-night kiss thing."

"I'll think about it," Addy said.

At home, she had to contend with her mother's con-stant complaining. Louise hated Frankie Ross and was not lax in expressing her feelings about him. "That boy is never going to amount to anything, Addy," she often told her daughter."

"Frankie is a very responsible boy, Louise," Clay would respond. "He holds a full-time job and is the only kid I trust to take my daughter out on my boat."

"You like him, because of his mother, Clay Connor. Why don't you just admit it? If he wasn't Sarah Ross's son, you wouldn't pay him any mind."

"That's simply not true, Louise," he said. "Adeline loves him and that's all I would need to know, if I didn't know him. That boy has more honesty and integrity, than anyone else I know."

"Well, if he marries our daughter, she'll be living in a two-bedroom clap-trap in New Roads for the rest of her life, having babies and red-beans and rice for dinner every night."

Clay stopped talking to his wife, just quit interacting and responding to her. He spent most nights at home reading or watching television in silence. Louise, however, was not impeded by his reluctance to converse with her on a regular basis. She continued to voice her displeasure with him, with Frankie Ross, and his mother, and with anything else her husband said or did.

His bitterness toward his wife only added to his fundamental disappointment with his own life. The life he was living was not the one he'd envisioned for himself. Even after he married Louise, he had intended to have a happy marriage, and a happy life. He was well-off, what most folks would consider rich, but that only mildly assuaged his bitterness for the way things had turned out for him. He only touched her, sexually, when his physical need overrode his revulsion for her.

Located on Highland Road, south of the school, was a popular bar and seafood restaurant, called The Cotton Club. The Cotton Club prided itself on its fried seafood, crabmeat au gratin, and bloody marys. The draft beer was affordable, for most college kids, and the crowd itself was the best entertainment.

It was to The Cotton Club that Addy agreed to go with Cherry and her date, Rob Michaels and his friend Jerry Gregory. They went in Addy's car, at her insistence, so Addy could leave and go back to her room if things got out of hand. The two men were at a table when Addy and Cherry arrived. Both of them stood up when the girls approached the table.

"Addy, this is my boyfriend, Rob, isn't he gorgeous?"

Addy nodded.

"And his friend is Jerry, Jerry Gregory. Jerry, this is Addy Connor."

"Hello, Addy," Jerry said, "I'm glad you decided to come along with Cherry."

"Thank you, Jerry," Addy replied and smiled at him. "I'm happy to meet you."

"Have a seat, girls," Rob said, "you both want a beer?"

"I'll have a beer," Cherry said, "how about you, Addy, you want a beer?"

Addy nodded.

"What kind of beer you want, beautiful?" Jerry asked her.

"I don't know, I don't drink very much…how about Dixie beer?"

"Dixie is horse-piss, Addy," he said, "How about a Budweiser?"

"That's fine."

"Bud Light, okay?"

"Bud Light," she said, nodding her head.

"Where are you from, Jerry?" Cherry asked him.

"Same place as Rob," he said, "St. Louis. Rob and I went to high school together."

They ordered the four beers, and everyone started looking at the menus to decide what they wanted to order.

The four of them got the catfish, with a crabmeat salad and French fries.

The place was noisy, so noisy they could barely hear each other. Cherry and Rob got up to dance, and Jerry asked Addy to dance.

He pulled her close to him and held her tightly. Addy was a little uncomfortable, but not so much that she complained. "You're beautiful," he told her.

"Thank you," she responded.

"You know it, don't you?"

"I know I'm not ugly, but I don't really see myself as beautiful."

"Well, you better start, because I'm going to tell you every time I see you."

"Well, thank you again," she said.

He pulled her closer and kissed her. She was not expecting it but didn't pull away for fear it would cause a scene. He released his lips from hers and kissed her cheek.

"That was incredible, Addy," he said. "I hope I didn't offend you."

"It's okay, I just wasn't expecting it."

"I'll let you know, the next time, Okay?

"Okay," she said, smiling at him.

"I'm going to kiss you again," he said and placed his lips back on hers. This time he was kissing her with passion and purpose.

Addy pulled her lips away from his. "It's customary to ask permission," she said.

"May I kiss you again, Addy?"

"No, you may not. I want to go back to the table."

"Did I make you mad?"

"I'm not mad. I just want to go back to the table." They started back toward their table.

"I'm going to take a leak," Jerry said. Addy went to the table and sat down. Rob was sitting there by himself.

"Did he get too pushy with you, Addy?"

"A little," she said, "he took me by surprise. I wasn't expecting it."

"I was watching, Jerry can be an asshole, sometimes. He didn't hurt you, did he?"

"I've been kissed before," she said, "but I usually see it coming."

"I can't blame him for wanting to kiss you, but he should mind his manners."

"Where is Cherry?" Addy asked.

"In the bathroom," he said, pointing in the direction of the ladies' room. "She's had too much to drink."

"Already, we haven't been here that long."

"She can't drink very much, I guess."

"Maybe I should go and check on her."

"She's coming out now," he said.

Cherry came back to the table and sat down.

"I think you've had enough, Cherry," Rob told her.

"No, I want another beer," she insisted loudly.

"I don't date drunks, Cherry, you've had enough to drink."

"Then take me to your apartment and screw my brains out."

"I'll do that when you sober up," he said, "I think Addy should take you home and get you into your bed."

"But I want to go to bed with you, Rob."

"Come on, Cherry, let me take you home," Addy implored her. "You need to sleep this off."

"You guys can come to our place and spend the night," Jerry said.

"I'm going home," Addy told him, "and I think Cherry should come with me."

"I do too," Rob said, "I'll help you get her into your car, Addy."

Addy managed to get Cherry into the dorm and to their room. Cherry went to the bathroom and threw up, then staggered to her bed, fell onto it, and went to sleep, without taking off her clothes.

Rob called about an hour later. "Did you get her to bed?" he asked.

"It wasn't easy," Addy said, "she threw up and then went to bed."

"I want to apologize to you, for my friend's behavior. He was an ass."

"It's okay, Rob, I still had a good time."

"I'm glad you did, and I'm hoping you'll go out with us again, maybe with just Cherry and me."

"I'd like that," Addy said.

Jerry was sullen when he and Rob got back to their apartment. "I wanted to tap that girl, Rob, why didn't you tell them to come here?"

"Because you were an asshole to her, Jerry. That girl is not used to being manhandled, you can tell by looking at her. She didn't like you kissing her like that, without any warning or invitation."

"I couldn't help myself," Jerry said, "she felt so good. Dammit, Rob, she felt really good, I gotta get her into bed."

"Then you might want to consider changing your strategy. Ask her, Jerry, don't force yourself on her. Addy has class, Addy 'is' class. She's not the girl for you, take my word for it."

"When I get in her pants, she'll be the girl for me, and I will get in her pants."

"No, you won't, Jerry, not this one. That girl is not like all the other girls you go with."

"What the hell are you talking about, Rob?" Jerry looked at him, perplexed, "I don't get it."

"Just leave her alone, that's all you have to get."

Jerry paused for a moment and then it clicked. "Oh, fuck me, why didn't I see this sooner? Of course, that's it. You like her, don't you, you've got a thing for Addy."

"It's not that, Jerry, I just don't like to see girls treated that way."

"Well, what the hell, I'll swap with you. You give me the blonde bimbo, with the big tits and I'll let you have Addy."

"Cherry is not mine to give away, Jerry, and Addy sure as hell not yours to trade."

"Okay, I'll cut you some slack, pal, I'll only screw her once and then I'll throw her away."

"Fuck off, Jerry," Rob said, "go to sleep."

Addy had dinner with her dad on a Wednesday night at The Village, an upscale Italian restaurant on Airline Highway.

"Your mother is worried about you, baby, you

should give her a call," Clay told his daughter.

"She always wants to talk an hour or longer, and it uses up my phone card."

"Then come home for a weekend and see her, and me, we both miss you."

"Okay, Daddy, I'll come home next weekend. I want to see Frankie, anyway."

"I see Frankie every so often. He's always working. I've been meaning to invite him to lunch, one day, but he's always busy."

"He's a busy guy," Addy said.

"So, how is school going for you?"

"It's hard sometimes, but I'm starting to enjoy it, I went on a double date with my roommate and her boy-friend, and his friend."

Clay's eyebrows went up, he wasn't sure he'd heard her correctly. "You did what?"

"Relax, Daddy, it wasn't like a real date, it was just dinner out at a local restaurant."

"I'm really surprised that you would do that. Did you tell Frankie about it?"

"I'm not going to, because I probably won't do it again."

"You 'probably' won't?" he said. "I'm not sure I like the sound of that, Adeline."

"I'm not doing anything wrong," she insisted, per-haps as much to convince herself as to assure her father of the fact. "Besides, what Frankie doesn't know, won't hurt him."

"That's a hell of a thing to say, baby, that's not my daughter talking. Who are you, young lady, and what have you done with Adeline?"

"Oh, spare me the melodrama, Daddy. I went out to dinner with a guy. I'm not sleeping with him."

Addy began to ponder the incident with Jerry Gregory. His kisses felt good, and had he not been such an oaf, she would have enjoyed the evening out. But what struck her more, was Rob's interaction with her. Rob seemed so much more mature than his friend, Jerry. Rob was calm and in control, he did not impress her as a guy who would force himself on a girl. She knew why he was attracted to Cherry. Cherry was good-looking and easy. Addy decided she would not go out with Jerry again. He assumed too much, and she figured him for a guy who didn't take rejection very well.

"Are you going to see Jerry again?" Cherry asked her.

"I don't think so," Addy replied, "he's too pushy."

"Rob wants us to go to a mixer with him, just the two of us, no Jerry."

"That's not really my style, Cherry, those events can get pretty rowdy."

"It's just guys meeting girls, that's what it's all about," Cherry said.

"But I have a guy. I'm not looking for a guy."

"It's just fun, Addy, you are not required to go to bed with every guy who expresses an interest in you. Yes,

Jerry is a troglodyte, you don't have to see him anymore, if you don't want to, but I want you to go, to have some fun with me."

"I have to go home this weekend, but okay, I'll go to a mixer with you."

❡❡❡

Mike Gaudin was sitting at his desk, with his head down, when Frankie arrived early for work.

"Hey, Mister Mike, how are you this morning?" Frankie asked him.

"I'm tired, Frankie."

"I'm sorry," Frankie said, "do you want to go back home and rest a while?"

"It's not that, Frankie, I'm not tired because I stayed up too late. I'm tired because I'm sixty-five-years old, and I can't work like I used to."

"Can't you take it easy, for a while? I can manage the field work. You don't have to work so hard."

"How much am I paying you?"

"Three and a quarter, Mister Mike," Frankie said.

"I have an idea I want to run by you."

"Okay, what's on your mind?"

"How would you feel about running the company for me?"

"I'd like that very much," Frankie said, "but I don't know anything about running a company."

"I can teach you how to estimate, put proposals together, and how to sell our work."

"I think I can learn anything."

"I know you can, Frankie, that's why I asked you. You're always here when I need you, and you look out for the company."

"So, how would this work, I mean how do we start?"

"You'll come into the office and begin learning everything I just mentioned. Eventually, you'll have to get your master's license in Baton Rouge for our work there. We'll work under my license, like we're doing now, but you will need to be licensed, in case I check out."

"Check out, you mean if you die?"

"Yes, that's always a possibility."

"You don't plan on dying, do you, Mister Mike?"

"Well, yeah, everybody dies, Frankie."

"Yes, sir, I know that, but not everyone dies at sixty-five. You can't do that to me."

"Oh, okay then, I'll notify the Almighty that it will be a real inconvenience to us if he takes me out anytime soon."

Frankie started laughing. "That's not exactly the way I meant that."

"I know, and I don't have a premonition or a death wish, I just want you to be prepared. I'll put you on salary, at two hundred a week, you will keep driving the company truck, and working as many hours as you determine is necessary. You'll most likely have some weeks

that you work more than forty hours, but there are benefits to being on salary. If you have to take a day off, every
so often, you get paid, and you get paid on all holidays,
we take off. Are you okay with that?"

"Yes, Yes, sir, Mister Mike, I'm fine with that. If
you feel confident that I can do this, I'll give it all I've
got."

"I know you will, Frankie, and, for goodness sake,
stop calling me Mister Mike. Call me Mike, we're part-
ners."

"You can quit work now, Mom," Frankie told his
mother, after telling her of his offer to run the company.

"Not on your life, son," she said. "You need to save
your money for when you get married."

"But that won't be for another two years."

"Save your money, Frankie, that time will come a lot
faster than you think."

℘℘℘

Clay Connor maneuvered his boat into the boat
house, attached the lift cables, and raised it up out of the
water. Louise was standing on the dock, when he came
out of the boat house.

"Why do you never take me out on the boat, Clay?"
she asked him.

"It's the only time I can be alone to think, about the
business, and the kids, and about you, without any dis-
tractions."

"I want you to take me out with you."

"I just got in. I don't want to go back out right now. How about tomorrow, maybe?"

"I was just thinking how much fun it would be, if you would take me out to the deep water and let me give you oral pleasure."

He looked at her smiling coyly at him for a few moments then let out a deep sigh. "Go put on your swim suit, I'll lower the boat."

She squealed, like a teenager and started running for the house. A few minutes later, she returned, in her swim suit and a light jacket.

When they returned, she was giddy. "Will you take me to bed now?" she asked him, almost pleading with him.

"Sure," he said, "I'll take care of the boat later."

There had been moments like that in their marriage over the years, moments that made him believe, even hope, that he could live happily with Louise. The shine always wore off, however, and he would drift back into melancholy.

Why is it, he often wondered, *that a man cannot be happy with what he has?* It seemed to him to be a universal condition, that people were never happy with what they had. Louise was not an unattractive woman, physically speaking, and, were it not for the woman she was, he could have loved her deeply and been happy. Men were visually incline. They fell in love with women because of the way they looked. It was a shallow thing, but real. Clay had seen men, married to women who were not pretty, and they were happy. And conversely, he knew men with beautiful wives who were miserable.

Why did he love Sarah Mayeux? He often forgot that she had married another man, and her name was now Sarah Ross. But she was still the same woman he'd loved for so long. When he first met Sarah, he thought she was the most beautiful creature he had ever seen. Frank Ross thought so too, apparently. Was Sarah just his ideal woman, the one who got away and could never be retrieved? He was told once, the teller of the fact being lost to his memory now, that every man had a secret love. It might be like Sarah was to him, or just a fantasy that would never be realized. But there was that one woman, out there somewhere in the world, that a man believed would make his world perfect. If he could just have her, marry her, and live with her, instead of the one he had, they would live happily ever after. He wasn't sure he believed that anymore. He was forty-one-years old, and he felt like life was passing him by.

೭ನ೭ನ

Addy and Cherry found the Phi Alpha Delta fraternity house, parked the car, and went inside. It was saturated with young, future lawyers, most of them drunk or on their way to being drunk. There was an equal number of girls circulating through the premises, indulging in free drinks and inane conversation. Addy felt out of place in the mix. She had worn her only party dress, a black sheath, belted in the middle, that came down to several inches above her knees, and her sandals.

"Stay as far away from me as possible, Addy," Cherry said.

"Why, Cherry, why would you not want to hang out with me?"

"Because you are freaking beautiful, that's why. Nobody is going to notice me with you in the room."

"I doubt that," Addy said, "you have Rob and, even if you didn't, you're a hottie."

"I don't have what you have," she said, "big boobs only get you so far." Before they could finish their conversation, Jerry Gregory appeared from out of the crowd. "You want to dance?" he asked.

"I don't think so, Jerry," Addy said.

"I wasn't talking to you, I want to dance with her," he said, pointing at Cherry.

Cherry's eyebrows went up in puzzlement, but she went with him to the dance floor. Addy was both relieved and a bit miffed. She wanted to tell him no, and he had taken that simple pleasure away from her. Several guys approached her, asking her to dance.

"I want to settle in a bit, first," she told them, "I'd like to dance later, if you still want to."

She got a drink from the bar, and it was much too strong for her. It was obvious that the bartenders had been told to go heavy on the alcohol, for the girls.

"Can you put some more coke in this, for me," she asked the one who had made the drink for her.

"Yes, I can, gorgeous," he said and complied with her request.

She noticed that Cherry was making out with Jerry on the dance floor.

Cherry and Jerry, she chuckled at the possibility of the two of them getting together. But it only lasted a short time, and Cherry was back to where Addy was, fuming over something.

"What's wrong, did Jerry step on your toes?"

"That sonofabitch, he wanted to dance with you, but when you said no, he quickly said he wasn't talking to you."

"That's pretty sneaky, all right," Addy said. "But I saw you making out with him."

"I like being kissed, and he is a good kisser. He only wants to get in my pants, though, and I demand at least a little obligatory pampering before I go to bed with a guy."

"Better thee than me," Addy said, and Cherry drifted off to another part of the house.

One of the guys who had asked Addy to dance, returned and asked her again. "Yes," she said, "I'd like to dance with you."

"I'm Aaron," he said, as they began dancing, "what is your name?"

"I'm Adeline," she said. "But I go by Addy."

"That's a beautiful name, for a beautiful girl," he told her.

"Well, thank you, Aaron," she told him. The dance ended, and they walked off the floor.

"I don't want to hog all your time," he said, "but I'd like to dance again, later, if you don't mind."

"Of course, Aaron, I'd like that." It was no longer than ten minutes and Aaron was back, asking Addy to dance, again. They had just started dancing when Jerry walked up to them. "Take a hike, pal, she's with me."

"No, I'm not," Addy told him forcefully. "I'm dancing with Aaron."

"He's an upper classman," Aaron said and left her standing there with Jerry.

"Come on," he said, taking her hand and pulling her along with him. He took her to a small room, in the back of the house. "You're teasing me," he shouted at her.

He put his arms around her, pulling her tight against him, and began kissing her. He was not kissing her gently, but like a man fully aroused, hard and desperately. She felt his tongue in her mouth and struggled to get free from him.

"Stop," she yelled, after managing to get her lips off of his, "Stop, Jerry, let me go." She realized that he was not going to stop and started to panic.

Suddenly, she felt him being thrown away from her. He landed on the floor a few feet away. Rob was standing over him, punching Jerry, while he was still on the floor. "I told you to leave her alone, you piece of shit," he screamed at his friend, who was trying to avoid the blows and get to his feet. Rob kept hitting him until Cherry grabbed him from behind and tugged on him. "Stop, Rob," she pleaded, "you're going to kill him."

Rob backed off and Jerry managed to stand up. "You take the side of a cunt, over your best friend?"

Rob knocked him to the floor again. "I told you to leave her alone, Jerry, why couldn't you just leave her alone?"

A small crowd had gathered and there was much murmuring, people asking what happened, and wanting to know who beat the hell out of whom.

Cherry was seeing about Addy and began walking her out to the car. She drove Addy's car back to the dorm, and they went to their room.

"That was a rude awakening," Cherry said.

"I know," Addy replied, "who would have thought Jerry would go that far? He scared the hell out of me."

"Looks like I have to find me another boyfriend," Cherry said with resignation.

"Why, Cherry? I thought you were crazy about Rob."

"I am crazy about him, but did you not catch what happened tonight?"

"Jerry was trying to force himself on me, and Rob stopped him"

"There was more to it than that, Addy, do you seriously not know?" Just then the phone rang, and Chery picked up. "Yes, oh hey, what's up? She's okay, just a bit rattled." She listened for about a minute. "Yeah, well, I sort of figured that out, yes, I understand. Okay, I'll ask her to come down. That was Rob, he's in the lobby, downstairs. He wants you to come down and talk to him."

"Really? But you told him that I'm okay. Why does he want to talk to me?"

"Just go, and talk to him, will you, please?"

Rob stood up when he saw Addy get off the elevator. He put his hand on her shoulder. "Are you okay?" he asked her.

"I'm fine, Rob, thank you for coming to check on me. He didn't hit me, I think he might have bruised my lips, but he was kissing me, hard, and squeezing me. I was really scared. I just don't understand why he did it."

"He's an asshole, Addy, that's why he did it. I threw him out of my apartment, made him pack up all his things and leave."

"Where did you come from? He was starting to hurt me, and then you were there. How did you know?"

"Cherry saw him dragging you into the back of the house. She came and got me, I was going over some business with the house manager."

"Well, thank you again, I really appreciate it," she said.

"That's not all I wanted to talk to you about," he said, "can we sit on the couch?"

"Sure," Addy said, a bit confused, and she followed him to one of the couches in the lobby. He sat down next to her.

"I'm a little out of my element, here, Addy. I've never done this before." He took a deep breath and exhaled slowly. "I knew this the first time I met you, but I thought it would go away. It hasn't gone away."

She looked at him, still trying to figure out where he was going with the conversation.

"I know you have a boyfriend back home, and I know you've made serious plans with him, but the truth is, Addy, that I've fallen for you. I've never felt this way, before, about anyone. You're perfect, you're beautiful, you're decent, smart, and everything I've ever wanted in a woman. What I'm trying to tell you, and not doing a very good job of it, I'm afraid—"

"You're doing fine, Rob," Addy said.

"I love you, Addy, I am in love with you. I don't know how it happened so quickly, I just know it did. If you will give me a chance, I'll prove it to you."

Addy drew a deep breath and blew it out, puffing up her cheeks in the process. "Wow, I have to be honest, Rob. I did not see that coming. I kind of thought you liked me, after the time at The Cotton Club, when you said you couldn't blame Jerry for kissing me. But I'm not sure how I feel yet, about you, I mean. Other than the obvious. You're still a mystery to me."

"The obvious?" he said.

"You're drop-dead gorgeous," she said.

"Now wait a minute," he said, "that's my line."

"I'd like to see what this is all about, and where it might go."

"That's all I'm asking you to do, Addy, will you have dinner with me tomorrow night?"

"Okay, yes, I will." She had forgotten that she had promised her folks, and Frankie, that she was coming home for the weekend. She didn't know what she was doing, but it made her feel new and alive. Life had thrown her a curve, and she had decided to swing at it.

Addy thought it more prudent to not make up a story about why she didn't come to New Roads that weekend. She decided that she would just not show up, and would think up a reason, when the time came.

Cherry was sitting on the side of her bed, when Addy returned from the lobby. "Tell me about it," she told her.

"He's in love with me," Addy said.

"Well, no shit," Cherry exclaimed, "I could have told you that the first night we went out with them."

Addy was tormented over what she should do. Life was moving too fast for her, all of a sudden. She spent all day Saturday in her room, trying to get a grip on her feelings. She loved Frankie Ross and had come to accept that, one day, they would get married and have a family. And now a man had come along, professing his love for her. She couldn't deny that she was attracted to Rob

Michaels. He was handsome, intelligent, and going to be a lawyer. What was there about him that a girl would not like?

She was experiencing feelings she never imagined she would be having, at this point in her life. If Rob was seriously in love with her, as he told her, it would complicate everything in her life. She almost hoped that Rob was lying to her to get her into bed. If he took her to bed, and then dumped her, it would solve her dilemma. She could go home to Frankie, keep her secret infidelity to herself, and live happily ever after, proverbially speaking.

"I have a surprise for you," Rob told her, after he'd picked her up, and stated driving to the restaurant.

"Where are we going?" she asked.

"Chalet Brandt," he said, "it's a very refined gourmet restaurant, French cuisine, really Continental, if you know what I mean."

Addy giggled. "I love it already."

"Tell me about yourself," he urged as they waited for their food. "You're from a small town?"

"Less than five-thousand people," she said. "New Roads lies along the banks of False River. False River is actually a big lake It was formed when the Mississippi changed courses, back in 1722, and moved on, leaving False River all alone. I suppose it was wondering if the big river was ever coming back."

"Well, that sounds like a sad story," he said, "and you grew up in New Roads?"

"I did, and my folks still live there, although my dad has an office for his business in Baton Rouge. Our house is right on the river, we have a dock and a twenty-six foot, Catalina, Bowrider boat. Do you know what a Bowrider is?"

"Yes, it's one of those boats, with the compartment in the front, for people to ride in, right?

"Yes, and it's a lot of fun. Oh, I have two older sisters, Marie and Cathryn, they're married and don't live in New Roads. What about you, you're from St louis?"

He nodded, my folks are pretty well-off, but my old man is the old-fashioned type. He's paying for my education, but he's made it clear that I'm going to have to earn my own living, after I graduate. That's why I decided to be a lawyer."

"So, you'll go to law school at LSU?" Addy said.

"I hadn't planned to go to LSU, initially, but I also didn't plan on meeting you and falling in love."

"I didn't plan on meeting you, either, it's a bit sudden and confusing."

"I certainly didn't intend to complicate things for you, but I had to be honest with you."

"I'm glad you were. I like you, Rob, I like you a lot, and I am attracted to you. We need to find out if this thing is real."

His car had a bench seat, and she slid over next to him. "There is a place in Tiger town, called The Chimes, it's a pretty cool bar and restaurant. I'd like to take you there, maybe next time, but, if you want to go now, we can."

"Let's go to your place," she said.

"Okay," he said, nodding his head.

In his apartment, she came up to him and wrapped her arms around him. He kissed her, gently and tenderly, caressing her shoulders. He kissed her face, cheeks, and forehead, and then her lips again. Addy melted in his arms and felt her legs get weak.

"I love your lips, Addy," he said, "I love everything about you. I need you but I'm not going to pressure you to do anything you don't want to do."

"I want you to make love to me, Rob," she said, "I have to know if what I'm feeling is real."

He picked her up and carried her to his bedroom, put her down, and started kissing her again. They helped each other out of their clothes and lay down in the bed next to each other.

His lovemaking was like nothing Addy had ever experienced or imagined could ever happen to her. He would stop, momentarily, and kiss her lips, softly and lovingly for a minute or so, until he felt her body start to move against him. Then he would continue loving her. Addy thought, for a moment, that she was going to pass out. She clutched at him and grabbed the hair on the back of his head. When he finished, she whimpered and called his name out loud.

It was a half hour before they could speak clearly. She lay in his arms, in disbelief of what had just happened to her. He had his arms around her, caressing her gently. Finally, he spoke."

"Well, that confirms it for me, Addy, not that I needed any confirmation."

"It was wonderful," she said. "Ohmigod, Rob, you were wonderful, I've never felt like that before."

"It was the most incredible thing that's ever happened to me, Addy," he told her.

"So, do you still want me to be your girl?"

"I want you to be my wife, Addy, I love you."

"I love you, too, Rob," she said, and lay her head back down on his chest.

CHAPTER 5

Coming of Age

Cherry heard the door being unlocked and threw the covers off. Addy walked into the room with a pleasant look on her face.

"You did it, didn't you?" Cherry said, smiling.

"Does it show?" Addy said.

"Well, yeah, the look on your face and the fact that you're coming home at eleven o'clock in the morning."

"I can't believe what has happened to me."

"I knew it was going to happen," Cherry said. "The first time we went out. He couldn't take his eyes off you. As drunk as I was, I knew it. I was mad at you a little, for a day or two, but you can't help being you."

"I'm really sorry, Cherry, I don't know how it happened. It's like a dream."

"Don't be sorry for me, Addy, I got what I wanted from Rob. I never believed it would be a long affair. I became extinct the moment he laid eyes on you."

"I don't know what I'm going to do. I almost wish he had just used me and then dumped me, although it would have broken my heart."

"He's not going to dump you, take my word for that. Did he seem distant, or in a hurry to take you home, this morning?"

"He made love to me again this morning."

"Well, there you go, roommate, the man is in love. You're every man's ideal woman. But how do you feel about him?"

"Ohmigod, Cherry, I love him. May God forgive me, but I love him. He made me feel, like I've never felt before."

"Then that complicates things for you, I assume.

"I don't know how I'm going to do this. This is going to hurt Frankie, and that's the last thing in the world I ever wanted to do."

"Well, you're a big girl now, Addy. This is the hard part of falling in love."

Addy waited a couple of days and went to see her father, at his office.

"This is a pleasant surprise, baby, to what do I owe this visit from my favorite daughter?"

Addy smiled and then had to fight back her tears.

"What's wrong, honey, are you okay?

"I have to tell you something, Daddy, no, I'm not pregnant," she interjected. He breathed a little easier. "I've met someone, a guy, and I love him. He loves me too, and I don't know how I'm going to tell Frankie."

"My God, Addy, how could this happen? This will destroy Frankie. You've been planning to marry Frankie Ross since you were fifteen years old."

"I know, Daddy, I don't know how it happened, it just did." She told him everything that had happened between her and Rob, excluding details of their lovemaking, about Jerry, and the mixer and how Rob had beaten Jerry up to protect her. "I fell in love with him and I know it's real."

"Okay, baby, I believe you, love does strange things to people sometimes. I certainly can understand why he would fall in love with you. I just hope he's uh…"

"He's not just trying to get in my pants, Father. He is in love with me, I know that. He wants to marry me."

"Who is he, Addy? Tell me about him."

"His name is Rob Michaels, he's from St Louis, his family is well off, but he's not pampered. Rob is in his senior year of pre-law. He will start law school this coming season."

"I'd like to meet him," Clay said, "ask him to come to my office any day this week."

"Okay, thank you, Daddy, for not being mad at me."

"I don't get mad at you, baby, you're my favorite daughter."

"I'm not going to ask you to move in with me, until were married, Addy," Rob told her. "I don't want people to get the wrong impression of you, or our relationship."

"My dad will be happy to hear that. He's kind of old fashioned."

"All dads are old fashioned," he said, "Did you tell him about us?"

"I did, and he wants to meet you, he said to ask you to come to his office."

He handed her a notepad. "Write down the address for me and I'll go see him."

"He'll be there every day this week," Addy said.

"I'm going now, come on, I'll drop you off at your room."

"You're going now?"

"Yes," Rob said, "I want him to know I'm serious."

He found the address, of the Connor business, parked his car, and walked into the lobby. The woman at the reception desk spoke to him.

"Can I help you, sir?" she asked.

"Yes, I'm here to see Mister Connor."

"Do you have an appointment, sir?"

"He's expecting me," Rob said.

"What's the name?"

"Robert Michaels."

She punched a button on her intercom, and Clay answered. "Yes, Julie, what is it?"

"There's gentleman here to see you. His name is Robert Michaels."

"I'll be right out," he said, and a moment later he entered the lobby, walked over to Rob, and extended his hand. "Hello, Mister Michaels," he said, "I wasn't expecting you so soon, but I'm happy to meet you. Let's go to my office."

Rob followed him to his office. In the office, there were two easy chairs sitting across from each other. Instead of sitting down behind his desk, Clay sat in one of the easy chairs, and motioned for Rob to take the other one, which he did."

"My daughter referred to you as Rob, so I assume you go by Rob."

"Yes, sir, Mister Connor," he said, "I go by Rob."

"Well, Rob, and by the way, please call me Clay," Rob nodded. "I won't pretend I was not surprised by my daughter's revelation that you and she are pretty serious about each other."

"I know it seems crazy, Mister Connor, Clay, I mean. We've only known each other a few months. So, I wanted to come see you, right away, to assure you this is not a flash in the pan thing, that is not going to fade away when school is out. I know about the guy back at home, Addy told me, she wanted to be upfront."

"She has to tell him, sooner or later. If this thing between you is real, and I've seen nothing that suggests to me it's not, I hope she will tell Frankie soon. You see,

Rob, Frankie Ross and I are good friends. His dad died in a car wreck when Frankie was twelve years old, and I have sort of taken him under my wing. He's a good man, and, I'll be honest. I was looking forward to having him as my son-in-law. But my primary concern is my daughter's happiness."

"That is my concern, as well, Clay. If I were not helplessly in love with Addy, I wouldn't be here. I loved her the first time I laid eyes on her, and I got so desperate that I went to her dorm, asked her roommate to ask Addy to come to the lobby and talk to me. I told her how I felt, and asked her to consider her feelings for me. She tells me she loves me."

"She convinced me that she does, Rob," Clay said. "What are your plans, for the future, I mean?"

"I changed my plans to go to Harvard Law and plan to get my law degree from LSU. I want to marry Addy this coming school year, she'll be a junior, and I'll be starting my post graduate work. So, we'll be in Baton Rouge for at least three-years. Then, I'd like to go back home, to St Louis and begin my career. If Addy wants to stay in Louisiana, we'll stay here."

"That's very considerate of you, Rob. I would have thought you'd insist on going back home, after you finish law school."

"Addy is my home now, Clay," Rob said.

Clay stood up, and Rob followed his lead. He took Rob's hand and shook it. "Then I'll be proud to have you for my son-in-law, Rob, thank you for coming."

"I love your dad, Addy, in a different way, of course," he told her after he had picked her up at the dorm.

"So, I assume it went well," she said.

"I have his blessing."

"Good, I'm happy for that."

"Now, we have to discuss the most pressing issue." Rob said.

"Where to go for dinner?"

"No, Addy, you have to tell Frankie about this."

"I know," she said, "I don't know how to do this, Rob."

"I can't go with you," he said, "that would not be fair to the man."

☙❧☙

Justin Cormier, husband of Eve Cormier, the head of the New Roads' citizens action committee, pulled his car into the driveway of the Connor house, got out, and went to the door.

"Well, hello, Justin," Louise said, as she answered the doorbell, "what can I do for you?"

"Eve asked me to bring these flyers over to you," he said.

"Oh, yes, she said she was sending them to me. You look hot, would you care for some iced tea?"

"I believe I would," he said. "is Clay around?"

"My husband is spending the weekend in Baton Rouge. He has a heavy workload, or so he said."

"I can't imagine, a man leaving a woman like you alone, Clay must be touched in the head."

"You're such a flirt, Justin," she said, smiling at him, "you're always saying things that make me feel good, thank you."

"You're a beautiful woman, Louise, I wish my wife was like you."

"Now, that's a terrible thing to say, Justin, Eve is a wonderful lady."

"She's a gossipy bitch, and you know it, Louise."

"Ouch," Louise said, "she does talk a lot, but I wouldn't call her a bitch."

"Oh, I know I went too far but, when I see a man like Clay with you, I just think about how much better my life could have been. I'm sorry, Louise," he said, "I just have this thing for you. I don't mean anything by it."

Louise thought about what the man had said to her. She knew he was probably just horny, but she had craved attention from her husband for so long that Justin's lame attempts to seduce her were almost welcome. She had to practically beg her husband to make love to her, and to get him to take her out on his boat, she had to offer him oral sex.

Now, here was a man wishing she was his. It was bullshit, she knew, but it felt good.

"Clay just doesn't know how lucky he is to have a woman like you, Louise."

"Are you trying to get me into bed, Mister Cormier?"

"That would be like a dream come true, Louise," he said.

Her need for a man who wanted her, just for her, skewed her thinking. Louise was emotionally bereft of the love of a man who desired her, who needed her. She found herself between the sheets, of the bed in the guest room with Justin Cormier. She happily discovered that the forty-seven-year old man had the stamina of a teen-aged boy and was surprisingly well endowed.

He made love to her twice in the course of the afternoon and continued his sweet talk to her after they had finished. He then took a shower and left.

"I'm going to call you, Louise," he said, as he walked out the door, "just to talk, if you don't mind."

"I'd like that, Justin," she said.

For the first time in many years, Louise felt sexually and emotionally fulfilled. A man had made love to her and, instead of running off for some other purpose afterward, he had stayed and made her feel special. She knew she would eventually end up in bed again with Justin Cormier, and she started looking forward to it.

ꞅꞌꞅ

As she drove out of Baton Rouge, Addy was think-

ing how she was going to do what she had to do. She took
the longer route across the Huey Long bridge onto 190,
Airline Highway, to give her more time to think. She felt
like the most horrible person in the world, knowing she
was going to hurt a man who loved her and was still
planning to marry her. But she couldn't change her heart.
She couldn't stop loving Rob, even if she wanted to.

When she got home, she pulled her car around to the
back of the house. "Will you call Frankie for me, Daddy?"

"You have to do this, Adeline," he said, "I can't
break up with Frankie for you."

"I know, I just want you to call him, tell him I'm
home, and ask him to come over."

Reluctantly, Clay did as his daughter had asked him.
He called Frankie and told him Addy was home and
wanted to see him. About twenty minutes later, Frankie
rang the doorbell of the Connor home. Clay came to the
door.

"Adeline is at the boat dock, Frankie, can you walk
around?"

She was sitting on the end of the dock, staring out
over the river. She heard Frankie's footsteps and stood
up. There were tears in her eyes as Frankie approached
her.

"You're breaking up with me, aren't you?" he said.

Addy started sobbing. "I met someone, Frankie, I'm
so sorry. I can't marry you."

"I know, Addy, I knew it must be something like this."

"What do you mean, how did you know?"

"It wasn't hard. You're never in your room when I call you. You haven't been home in months, and, when I saw the look on your dad's face just now, I knew for sure."

"I'm sorry, Frankie, I truly am, I never wanted to hurt you."

You've broken my heart, Addy. I love you, I'll always love you. Even if I move on and marry someone else, I'll never stop loving you. I hope he makes you happy. I do want you to be happy, even if it's not with me."

He turned and walked away, without saying anything more. She stood on the dock, still sobbing, and watched him until he walked out of her sight. On Sunday night, she drove back to her dorm.

‹›‹›

Frankie said nothing, to his mother or at his work, that would indicate that his world had been torn apart. His demeanor did not change, he shed no tears, nor did he become angry. He had prepared himself for Addy's revelation to him. She had been avoiding him for months, and he was certain that could mean only one thing.

He had lied to her when he told her he wanted her to be happy. It seemed that was something they always say in movies. "If you really love her, you'll just want her to be happy." That was a fallacy. The scorned individual, more often or not, wanted his, or her, betrayer to be just as miserable as he, or she, was. In time, however, Frankie came to harbor only pleasant memories of the girl he'd loved all his life. But on this day, he felt little benevolence toward her.

"I have to tell you something, Mom," he said to her when she came in from work.

"What is it, honey?" she asked.

"Addy met someone at college and is going to marry him."

"Oh no, Frankie, I'm so sorry," she said. "Are you okay?"

"No, but I will be," he said.

Sarah found an old business card of Clay Connor's and called him at his office in Baton Rouge.

When Julie told him that Sarah Ross was on the line, he picked up immediately. "Sarah, I'm so sorry about what happened. I truly wanted my daughter to marry Frankie. But the heart of a young girl is fickle. They can leave a young man's heart shattered and broken. I hope he is okay."

She didn't know if his comment was a dig at her or just truth rising to the surface.

"Frankie is heartbroken, of course, Clay, he loves Addy very much. But life goes on, and he will too. I just called to tell you that I don't blame you or harbor any hard feelings toward you. You've always been good to my son, and I'm grateful to you for that."

"It's kind of ironic, isn't it, Sarah?"

"How's that?" she asked him.

"My daughter broke Frankie's heart, and his mother broke mine. I take no comfort in that. I mean, I don't consider it karma. And I truly wish it were not so."

"I'm sorry for the past, Clay, we can't change it, but I am sorry for hurting you."

"Thank you for calling, Sarah," he said, "it's always good to hear your voice."

Frankie Ross sent off for some study books, to prepare for his master electrician's exam. He studied for a month and then sat for the test in Baton Rouge. About a month later, he received confirmation that he had passed the test. Mike Gaudin was elated at hearing the news. He again asked Frankie about buying the business. He was convinced that Frankie Ross, with his youthful energy and drive, could grow the shop into a much bigger concern.

"I don't have a lot of money, Mike," Frankie told him. "I help my mom with the bills. I don't have any money to put down."

"I'll help you get a loan, son. You can use the company, and its assets for collateral. I'll get a list together of the inventory. Our greatest asset is the customer base. You'll have to replace the vehicles, in a few years, but if you maintain the customer base, and add to it, that will make you a good living."

"I want to do it," Frankie said, "If I can get a loan, I'll do it."

Mike's Electric Company in New Roads had almost a monopoly on all the electrical work performed in New Roads. Mike Gaudin had lived in New Roads all his life. He was well-liked and respected as an honest man. When word got out that he was selling his business to Frankie Ross, folks were inclined to continue doing business with the company. Frankie had acquired a good reputation for being honest and dependable.

Clay Connor called the loan manager at Peoples Bank and Trust, a man named Martin Aucoin (Oh-quinn).

"Hello, Clay, Martin answered, what can I do for you?"

"Martin, I'm calling to ask a favor. You know Mike Gaudin, who has the electrical company."

"Of, course, Clay, Mike has been doing business with us since were first established in new Roads."

"I figured that, Martin, he's in the process of selling his business to Frankie Ross."

"Yes, sir," Martin said.

"He's probably going to apply for a loan. I want to make sure he gets that loan."

"How much is he going to need, Clay?"

"Don't know for sure, at least fifty thousand. I heard that was how much Mike is willing to sell it for. Just to Frankie."

"It's worth a lot more than fifty grand, Clay."

"I know, but regardless, I want to guarantee his loan. I'll come in and sign paperwork, to that effect, but I don't want Frankie or Mike to know I'm doing this."

"I understand, Clay," Martin replied. "I'll keep you apprised of the situation."

"Thank you, Martin, call me when the paperwork is ready, and remember, don't say anything about this to anyone."

"I won't, Clay, thank you. I'll be in touch."

Frankie applied for a sixty-thousand-dollar loan. He needed fifty thousand to buy the business and the extra ten to replace the operating capital Mike Gaudin had in his business account.

"Give me a couple of days, Frankie, and I'll let you know if the loan is approved," Martin Aucoin told him.

Frankie was almost in a daze. He had never discussed money with anyone for more than a few hundred dollars. He was taking home close to a hundred and seventy dollars a week, which calculated out to roughly to about seven hundred and thirty-six dollars a month. He gave his mother two-hundred a month for bills and, since he'd lost Addy, he spent very little of his money on anything or anyone. There wasn't a lot to do in a town the size of New Roads, so he had saved a few thousand dollars. He had been planning to buy a new car, but Mike began letting him drive the company truck home, so, Frankie saved his money.

Martin Aucoin called Clay Connor and told him about the loan.

"Okay, Martin," Clay said, "if you will go ahead and approve it, I'll come in a sign the necessary paperwork."

"Holy cow, Mom, I got the loan," Frankie told his mother. "I've never even seen sixty thousand dollars, before. I'm not sure I can handle this."

"Of course, you can, son," she said, "my advice to you is to go talk to Clay Connor. Clay is the most successful businessman in town, and he will help you on how to move forward, take care of your taxes, withholdings, and anything else you need to know."

Frankie made the call, and Clay asked him to come to the Connor house the following Saturday. The place smelled like Addy, Frankie imagined. Her pictures were all over the living room.

"Let's go sit at the kitchen table, Frankie," Clay suggested. Frankie was relieved that there were no pictures of her in the kitchen. "You'll need a CPA, I suggest William Myers, your mother used to work for him a few years back. Billy will keep up with your taxes, file your report at the end of the year, and send out your W-2s. He can do your payroll for you but, honestly, you can do it yourself cheaper. How many employees do you have?

"I have five—six, with the warehouse guy, but he is also a helper."

"Do you have an office manager?"

"Yeah, me, and I am also the lead electrician. Mike

was the office manager but he had me to run the field. I don't have that luxury. I'll probably use an answering service, so I can call in from time to time during the work day and get messages. I drive one of the service trucks, so if there is an emergency call, I'll go and take care of it right away."

"If you grow the company, you may want to hire an estimator and act as your own company manager. You'll have to develop someone who can replace you in the field."

"That may be a while, yet," Frankie said.

"It will take time, but just keep in mind that you won't be able to do everything yourself. You will have to learn to delegate."

"I will, Clay, I'll remember that. It will be hard, but I'll do it. Thank you for all your help."

"No problem, Frankie, don't be a stranger. I know it's awkward for you with all that's happened, but I'd like for us to stay friends. Two businessmen can be friends and meet for lunch, every so often."

"I'd like that," Frankie said, "I really would."

芝芝芝

Justin Cormier continued his illicit affair with Louise Connor. She felt that meeting him at the Connor house was risky. Small towns have few secrets, so she insisted that they meet elsewhere. Louise gained more than mere sexual gratification from their rendezvous. And even the sexual gratification was more than mere. It was incredible and fulfilling for Louise. Justin was the husband of the woman she had come to detest and that brought immense satisfaction to Louise. Every time she went to bed with Eve's husband was payback for the woman's digs at her about Sarah Ross and Louise's husband."

Justin owned a fishing camp on the other side of the lake. He had fixed up the small house and it had become, for Justin, a way to stay away from his wife. He began meeting Louise at the camp, after too many ferry rides to a motel in St. Francisville.

"I can't take a chance on getting caught, Louise," he told her. "Do you have any idea what a shit storm that would stir up?"

"You could marry me, Justin," Louise said.

"I'd love that, Louise, but Eve would take half my business and all my money. You wouldn't want me if I didn't have a pot to piss in."

"I don't love you for your money, Justin. I only want your dick and your sweet talk. You make me feel alive again."

"Then it's yours anytime you want it, baby, we just have to be careful."

But the best laid plans of mice and men often go awry, as the saying goes. Frankie Ross had done electrical work at Justin's fishing camp cabin, and he knew the cabin well. It was not far off the road, not directly on the water. Justin Cormier's boat house and dock were a couple hundred feet or so from the house, at the water's edge. Frankie took notice of the house every time he drove down 413 to an estimate or a service call.

One fateful Wednesday morning, he approached Cormier's cabin from the north and spotted a familiar car parked behind the cabin. Justin's pickup was in the drive way, and the other car had been pulled up behind the cabin. Frankie recognized the car immediately as the gray 1988 Lexus LS 400 that Louise Connor drove.

"Holy shit," he said out loud. "Why would Louise Connor's car be parked behind Justin Cormier's fishing cabin?" he asked himself. There could only be one reason, he knew, but what should he do about it.

He wouldn't do anything, right away. He would wait until he saw the car back at the Connor house before he decided what to think or do. Perhaps they had sold the car. He hoped that was the case. But the next morning, the car was back in the driveway at her house.

Now, he had a crisis of conscience, what should he do? First, he wouldn't tell anyone, not even his mother. He would wait a while and then decide what to do.

CHAPTER 6

Riverbend

Frankie continued to watch Louise Connor. She didn't leave her house very often but, since Frankie lived within walking distance of the Connor home, he drove by there every morning. One morning, he noticed her car was gone from the house. It was around the same time of day he had passed the cabin and spotted her car the first time.

On an impulse, he drove around the lake and passed by Cormier's cabin. To his dismay, the Lexus was parked behind the house, and he could see Justin and Louise standing at the dock. They were obviously more than friends, for she was wrapped around him, and he was kissing her with what appeared to be great passion.

She's cheating on Clay, he thought. What should he do now? He knew if he told Clay, it would be a mess and would probably end their marriage. But how could he not tell him? Clay Connor was a friend and had always treated him like the son he'd never had. He placed a call to Clay at his office.

"Hello, Frankie," Clay said, "what can I do for you?"

"I'm going to be in Baton Rouge, a little later today, and I was wondering if I could drop in to see you."

"Of course, you can, Frankie, I'll be here all day, come any time."

Frankie arrived at Clay's office at around one o'clock, that afternoon.

"What's on your mind, Frankie?" Clay asked him.

"This is hard, Clay, telling you this, I mean."

Clay's brow wrinkled with concern and some measure of foreboding. "Just tell me, then," he said.

"I'm not making any accusations, please understand but, recently, I saw Mrs. Connor's car at Justin Cormier's fishing camp. I saw it twice in the past two weeks."

"Really," Clay said, "and you're certain it was my wife's car?"

"Yes, sir, the Lexus. I wish to God I was wrong, but that's what I saw. I struggled with it for a week, before I came here but I thought you should know."

"Have you told anyone else?"

"No, and I don't intend to."

"Well, thank you, Frankie, please don't mention this to anyone. I know it was hard for you to come and tell me this, but I do appreciate it."

After Frankie left his office, Clay picked up the phone and called a friend of his at the Aguillard (Ah-gi-ya) Detective agency. "Howard, this is Clay Connor. I have a job I need you to do for me."

e⁄ɔe⁄ɔ

During the 1992 Christmas holidays, Odell Ross passed away. He left his house and twenty-thousand dollars to Sarah. The house was not worth a lot of money and Sarah thought about keeping it for Frankie.

"I'd sell it, Mom," he told his mother. "I don't know if I want to live in Grandpa's house. There are a lot of bad memories in that house. Dad grew up in that house and I think of him every time I go visit Grandpa. So, unless you want me to leave, for some reason, I'd sell it if I was you."

"Why in the world would I want you to leave, Frankie?"

"Don't you ever want to get married again, Mom? Don't you ever just want to go out on a date with a man?"

"I told Tom Robillard, four years ago, that I would have dinner with him when you turned eighteen. He said he could wait that long, but then he married a woman he met in Morganza. So, I missed my chance, I suppose."

"Well, thank God, Mrs. Robillard came along and took him away from you," Frankie said.

Sarah laughed. "He wasn't much to look at, but he was a very nice man. I couldn't see myself marrying him, though. I imagine it would have gotten awkward after a while."

"I know you're lonely, and I hate to see you lonely. I'm not saying I think you should find a man. I just worry about you."

"I know you do, Frankie, and I appreciate it."

"I hear talk, Mom, nothing right out in the open, but comments, little comments about you."

"What do you hear, Frankie? I've never dishonored your father's memory, and I never will."

"That's not what I meant," he said. "A man at the restaurant was watching you. I don't think he knew if I could hear him or not, but he said, 'damn, that is one good-looking woman.'"

"That's really nothing," she said, "I get asked out quite a bit, but I just don't want to get onto that merry-go-round."

"Addy said her father is still in love with you."

"I expect he is, Frankie, but Clay is married, and I doubt he'll ever be not married."

"But you liked him, once, didn't you?"

"I thought I loved him at one time, but I met your father, and that settled that," she said.

"Do you think you could ever love him again?"

"What are you doing now, playing matchmaker for your mother?" she said, chuckling. "I don't think it's in the stars for Clay Connor and me to be together."

"He still loves you, Mom."

"I know," she said.

"That has to count for something," Frankie said.

That summer, Sarah paid off the ten-year note on the Riverbend acreage. It had taken all of the twenty thousand dollars, she had put in the bank from her husband's life insurance. The mutual fund, Fidelity Magellan, despite the stock market crash of 1987, had averaged almost twenty-nine percent annual growth. The twenty thousand dollars she had invested from the life insurance, plus the two-thousand Frank had started the account with had grown to a hundred and thirty-six thousand-dollars.

Sarah was almost in disbelief over Frank Ross's insight. He was either brilliant or just blind lucky, she thought. She preferred to believe that her husband was a financial genius. She realized, though, that if she cashed in the fund, she would have to pay taxes on the money, and that would reduce it by a substantial amount. She decided instead to begin drawing smaller amounts from the account for her living expenses. The fund would continue to grow, she hoped, and her withdrawals would not diminish her balance substantially. Her house was paid for and her personal expenses were not much.

With an influx of tourists and large numbers of people flooding into the county wanting to build vacation getaways or retirement homes along the river, the two acres Frank had bought in 1980 had appreciated greatly. Sarah believed it was time to put hers and Frank's plan into action.

Sarah quit her job at the restaurant and applied for a loan to build her fishing camp and boat rental business. She kept Odell Ross's house, thinking she might use it for collateral for the loan, and rented it out to a family in New Roads.

"You'll need a business plan, Mrs. Ross," the banker told her.

"I'm not sure how to do that, Mister Aucoin," she replied.

"Get estimates from a builder for construction of the facility you want to build. Estimate your operating costs for an amount of time you think it will be before the business starts earning money. I'll help you put it together."

⁊⁊

Knowing what he did, about his wife's ongoing affair with Justin Cormier, didn't help Clay, in his day-to-day interaction with Louise. The tension between them had gotten so bad that it seemed it would explode before too long. Only cursory conversation passed between them, and Clay began spending more time away from home, in his condo in Baton Rouge.

Eve Cormier became suspicious of her husband and was convinced that he was being unfaithful to her.

"I know you're cheating on me, Justin," she yelled at him one evening.

"You don't know any such thing, Eve," he responded.

"Then what do you do all day long? You're never in your office, where do you go when you disappear for hours on end?"

"I go fishing, Eve, I love to fish."

"Nobody fishes that much," she said.

"I do."

"Who is she, who are you seeing? I know you're seeing someone, and I want to know who she is."

"Fuck off, Eve," he growled back at her. "Leave me alone."

"I want a divorce, Justin," she told him.

"You're not getting my business, Eve, if that's what you think you're going to do."

"I'm entitled to half of it," she said.

"You'll never live to see it."

"Are you threatening me, Justin?"

"No, of course not, Eve, that would be against the law."

"You don't want lawyers to see your books because you've been doing underhanded business for years now."

"You don't know as much as you think you know."

"I know enough," she threw back at him.

Justin was not worried about his wife's veiled threats. They had been through this before. But he began to contemplate the possibility of getting out of his marriage. The Cormier marriage had been contentious for years. Justin's arrogance and sense of selfish entitlement had ripped them apart, and his wife's constant prattling about anything, and everything, that might be on her mind had done nothing to alleviate their animosity toward each other.

He knew he could not get a divorce. Louisiana divorce laws were archaic and burdensome. Eve was right, and she knew it. She would be able to take half his business. He would have to open up his books to prying eyes, and that he could not do. He had way too much money for the annual average receivables the business generated. And it was no small matter that he was sleeping with another man's wife. That fact, if ever exposed, would send him to the guillotine, if Louisiana actually used that means to discourage an adulterous man from continuing his devious ways. Justin chuckled as he pondered that thought. Nevertheless, if it were known about his affair with Louise Connor, it would cost him more than half his business.

"So, which one of these bitches am I gonna have to kill?" he jokingly said to himself.

Eve was the mother of his children, but their children had left home, bound for big cities and bigger opportunities, and had never returned. Louise Connor did things for him that he just couldn't put a price on. He certainly didn't want to marry Louise, a woman who would cheat on her husband could not be trusted was his assessment on that subject. Justin Cormier was a man in a crisis, however. The thought of losing his money, and never making love with Louise Connor again, was simply unimaginable to him. He called Louise and asked her to meet him at the cabin.

After they made love, Louise rolled over onto her pillow. "You must be under a lot of stress, Justin," she said. "You've never assaulted me, like that, with such passion."

"I've missed seeing you," he said.

"Is everything okay with you?"

"Everything is fine, like I said, I needed you really bad. I'm sorry if I was too rough."

"Don't be sorry," she said, "it was wonderful, it was incredible. It was really nice, Justin."

"I'm going to grill some steaks for us in the gazebo on the dock," he told her, changing the subject.

He baked two potatoes and then put two T-bones on the grill. Then he mixed them a drink. While the steaks were cooking, he sat down next to her on the couch and began kissing her again. She moved over onto his lap and began moving her hips against him.

"We can't do it here, Louise," he said, "what would the neighbors think?"

"But the gazebo is enclosed, who will see us?"

"Probably nobody," he said, "but the steaks will get cold. Let's eat first and then we'll go back inside."

They paid no mind to the small boat, sitting a couple hundred yards offshore, as they finished their meal and then walked, clinging to each other, back to the cabin.

ᥴᥱᥲᥱᥲ

Sarah Ross was busy getting her business plan in order. Martin Aucoin had given her an outline that showed her, in great detail, how to proceed with her plan.

"I'm going to need an estimate from you for wiring my building," she told her son, Frankie.

"Of course, ma'am," he told her. "There is no power to the property, so you'll need to contact the utility company and get the cost for them to set a transformer for you. I'd suggest we take the power to the building underground, instead of using an overhead service drop."

"I don't know what that means, Frankie," she said, laughing at his presentation. "You're so serious."

"You're a customer now, Mom," he said. "Why would I treat you any different than I treat my other customers?"

"Good point, Mister Ross, thank you. I'm going to need a plumber and an air conditioning guy, too."

"I can recommend some people for you to talk to," he told her. "And I'll help you oversee the work."

"How much will that cost me?" she asked, smiling at him.

"You're my mom. I won't charge you anything for helping you."

"Well, thank you, kind sir. I'm finally getting some payback for changing all those dirty diapers."

"I meant to thank you for that, Mom. I would have done it myself, but I just didn't know how."

"No problem," she said. "Are you okay, Frankie, I mean with what happened between you and Addy?"

"I'm not sure, at this point, that I'll ever be okay with it," he said. "But Addy is married now and that's reality. I heard she will be moving to St. Louis, next year, when her husband finishes law school."

"I'm so sorry, son, I know how it feels to lose someone you love."

"I've been dating Hanna Morley. She was in school with me and Addy. Actually, she was Addy's best friend."

"I'm glad to hear that," Sarah said. "Is it serious, between you? I mean do you love her, or ever think you'll love her? I'm sorry to pry in your personal life, but I worry about you."

"I'm never going to love anyone but Addy, Mom, not ever."

Hanna Morley was not an ugly woman, but neither was she a head-turner. She was, what many people would describe as plain looking, a generic term that is difficult to define. Hanna was five feet, four inches tall, and weighed 115 pounds, she had reddish brown hair and blue eyes. Hannah was light skinned, but shapely, and wore glasses. She had suffered in the shadow of Addy Connor for all the time the two girls were friends. Addy was beautiful and Hannah was not was the general consensus of most folks who knew them both.

Hannah was working at the diner on Main Street in New Roads when Frankie Ross started having lunch there. She made no secret of the fact that she was attracted to him. Frankie was only mildly interested in Hannah. He sensed that she would be easy to get into bed. The only negative about that, he surmised, were the unintended consequences. It could get complicated, and he had not been a sufficient amount of time without Addy that he was looking for a relationship.

The time came, however, that his need outweighed his caution. In more baser terminology, Frankie let his small head do his thinking for him, and he asked Hannah out on a date.

"Where do I pick you up, Hannah?" he asked her, after she had accepted his offer to, "take in a movie."

"I have an apartment on Hospital Road, do you know where that is?"

"Yes, I know where Hospital Road is, Hannah, everybody knows where Hospital Road is. Is that those apartments off the road, to the right?" he said.

"That's them," she said.

Not wanting to take her out in his work truck, Frankie borrowed his mother's car. He drove to Baton

Rouge and they had dinner at a Denny's Restaurant then went to a movie. It was ten o'clock when got back to her apartment.

"Do you want to come in, for a while?"

"If you want me too, I do," he said.

"Come on," she said and got out of the car. He got out quickly and followed her to the door. He found that when Hannah removed her eyeglasses, she was more attractive, almost pretty, he decided.

The next morning, he woke up in Hannah's bed. "Oh, shit," he exclaimed, after reaching for his watch on the nightstand. "I have to get my mother's car back to her."

"Can I see you again, Frankie?" she asked him.

"Sure, Hannah, I had a good time. I'll call you later."

"Thank you for last night."

"Thank you, Hannah," he said, as he put on his clothes, "I gotta go."

His mother was mildly amused but worried. "I was examining the scenarios, last night, when you didn't come home," Sarah said. "I figured the car broke down, in which case I would have gotten a phone call, then I worried about you being in an accident. That was the worst one, and then I said to myself, my boy is getting it on with Hannah Morley. Thank goodness it was that one. I do wish you'd call me though, Frankie, when things like this happen."

"I'm sorry, Mom," he said, "it just all went so fast,

five minutes after we went into her apartment, we were in her bed."

"Okay, son, I think that's all I need to know about that. Just call me next time, so I won't worry about you."

"I will, Mom, I'm sorry, again."

He and Hannah started dating regularly, and he slept over at her apartment more often than not. Hannah was really good in bed, very passionate and eager to please, he discovered, and he became quite fond of her. It was soon very clear to Frankie that Hannah was in love with him.

✂✁✂✁

Justin Cormier went to the police station and reported that his wife, Eve, had disappeared. "It's been three days since she left to go see her mother in Lafayette, and she never got there," he told the police.

They questioned him at great length and made him fill out a missing person's report.

A call to Eve's mother added new suspicions to the case. According to the mother, Eve had not mentioned to her that she was coming to see her. An APB—All Points Bulletin—was issued for Eve Cormier and her car. More suspicion fell upon Justin because of his mother-in-law's claim that Eve had not told her that she was coming to visit her.

"Aw, hell," Justin told them, "that crazy damned

woman is seventy years old and in the early stages of Alzheimer's. She can't remember her name half the time. My wife told me she was going to see her mother. I know she called her."

In an interview with Eve Cormier's mother, police confirmed Justin's claim regarding the woman's mental state. She seemed detached and unable to follow a conversation with any degree of concentration.

Eve's car was eventually discovered by some kids swimming in Bayou Courtableau (Cor-tob-la). It apparently had been driven off the wooden bridge that spans the junction between the bayou and Darbonne bay, about a half mile up river from the Bayou Courtableau Bridge on Highway 190. Subsequent lifting of the car from the water revealed that Eve Cormier's body was in the trunk of the car. She had been shot in the head.

Justin was visibly, and believably, distraught over the news of his wife's death. The state police became involved in the investigation. There were no recoverable fingerprints on the car, but an autopsy of Mrs. Cormier's body found a few strands of hair and skin that she had, most likely, ripped from her assailant's head and face.

The DNA was sent to the FBI facility in Washington, but no match was found in the data base.

The violent death of Eve Cormier was a shock to the small community of New Roads. A good many of the people who knew him were convinced that Justin Cormier was somehow involved in the crime. The manager of

Justin's bank notified the state police that Cormier had drawn ten-thousand-dollars from his checking account several days before his wife's disappearance.

The state police detective assigned to the case, a Captain Harmon, also believed that the woman's husband had something to do with his wife's death. "I can't prove it yet, but I will," he promised the New Roads sheriff.

While the entire town was concerned with the horrible crime that had been committed against one of their own, Clay Connor decided it was time to confront his wife, Louise, about her affair with Justin Cormier.

"I want a divorce, Louise," he told her, one afternoon across their kitchen table. At first, Louise was defiant upon hearing her husband's pronouncement.

"Then I want my house, and half of everything you own," she screamed at him, in a rage. "I've given you twenty-five years of my life, Clay Connor, and three children. You are not going to leave me penniless. I'm forty-four years old, how am I going to make a living?"

"Calm down, Louise, I'm not going to leave you penniless. First off, this house was in my family when we married. I grew up in this house and I'm not going to let you have it. Why would you want it, anyway? You know you're not going to stay in New Roads."

"Well, I just might," she said, "I've been here over half my life, I love it here."

"No, you don't, Louise," he said. "You think that Justin Cormier is going to marry you and you want to have this house."

"What?" she shot back at him, "What the hell are you talking about?"

"You're having an affair with Justin," Clay said.

"I most certainly am not Where in the world did you get that idea?"

He shoved a manila folder across the table to her.

She opened it and saw the pictures. Her face turned pale. "It's your fault, Clay, you never loved me, you never treated me like a wife. You only made love to me when I begged you to, and I had to give you a blow-job just to get you to take me out in the boat. It's all your fault." She was crying now.

"Okay, I'll concede that I was not a perfect husband, but you started bitching on our honeymoon, and you never stopped. Nothing is ever good enough for you, Louise. You're in a perpetual state of being pissed-off, all the time. You're just not pleasant to be around."

"But you loved me once, didn't you?" she said, almost like a little girl.

"I did," he said, "and it was good for a long time, but you wore me out."

"It started going bad when Frank Ross died. That woman was free then, and you've never given up hope that you will be with her, one day."

"That has nothing to do with us, Louise," he lied.

"I don't believe you," she said. "You still want her, don't you? Why can't you just tell me the truth?"

As much of a burden, as she had been to him, he couldn't tell her the truth. He didn't want to hurt her, despite the misery she had caused him. "I *am* telling you the truth, Louise, you just don't want to believe it. Anyway, we are going to end our marriage, and here is how it's going to happen. I'm going to keep the house and my business. You getting half the business is just not practical. I need to have a means of earning a living. I'll let you have the condo in Baton Rouge. It's easily worth two-hundred-grand. You'll sell it back to me, and I'll pay you the two-hundred-thousand in five annual installments of forty thousand dollars. I'll pay you alimony, enough for you to live on, until you remarry, if you ever do. But I want out free and clear."

"But what about these pictures, Clay?" she asked him.

"Those pictures are insurance," he said. "You are going to admit to adultery."

"I can't do that, Clay, what if it gets out?"

"It won't, Louise, this will be a private matter. The State of Louisiana requires a couple to remain separated for a year before the dissolution of their marriage. If adultery is involved, the separation time is six months. I want to be done with this in six months."

Louise reluctantly accepted his demands, although it hurt her very much. The ending of their marriage was terrifying for her. Clay had always taken care of everything in their lives. She had come to take it all for granted—

their lifestyle and no concern over money. She had no real responsibility, other than keeping the house up, cooking their meals, and buying clothes for the girls. Now, she would have to make decisions on her own, and she was intimidated by it all.

"I want to give you some advice, Louise," he said, "and this is not out of jealousy. But don't marry Justin Cormier. That would be a mistake. I believe that man is responsible for his wife's death, and I don't want the mother of my children to end up like Eve Cormier ended up."

The advice fell on deaf ears, however. A year later, Justin asked Louise to marry him, and she did. "Justin was just too good in bed, for me to pass up his proposal," she told her friends at the Ladies' Auxiliary. The thought that he might cheat on her never crossed her mind.

ⲉⳝⲉⳝ

Hannah Morley was deeply in love with Frankie Ross, and she possessed no inclination to keep it a secret. She stopped taking her birth-control pills, in hope that she would get pregnant and Frankie would marry her. She was two-months along, when she told him, one evening at her apartment.

"I thought you were on the pill, Hannah," he asked her.

"I forgot to refill my prescription one time, and I missed a few," she explained.

"Holy shit," he replied. "I wasn't ready for this, but don't worry. I'll take care of you and the baby. We'll have to get married, I guess. Do you even want to get married? To me, I mean."

"I would love to marry you, Frankie," she said. "I love you. I've loved you since high school."

"Really?" he said, "I didn't know that, Hannah, you never acted like you even knew me."

"You were with Addy, and I knew I didn't have a chance with you, so I just never let my feelings be known to you, or anyone."

"Well, then, I guess we should make it official." He took her hand in his, got down on one knee, and asked her, "Hannah Morley, will you marry me?"

"Yes, Frankie Ross, I will marry you, thank you for asking." She was beaming and almost in tears. "Now, will you take me to bed and screw my brains out?"

He chuckled, at her request and followed her into the bedroom.

They were married at the justice of the peace in New Roads. Frankie moved into her apartment with her, leaving his mother alone. Sarah offered to let them live in Odell Ross's house, as soon as it came available. Frankie declined, saying, "You need to sell that house, Mom, and use the money for your business venture. I'll get us a rental house, when the time comes, or maybe I'll buy a house."

In time, Hannah gave birth to a baby girl. They named her Penelope Lane, Lane being Hannah's father's name. Inevitably, the girl would be called Penny Lane. Only Frankie's mother, Sarah, had advised them of that eventual happenstance, neither Hannah nor Frankie being aware of that old song by The Beatles.

Frankie Ross had a daughter. He began to believe that he might actually find happiness in a world without Addy Connor, or whatever her name was now.

CHAPTER 7

Moving On

Fair Oaks Drive, a house in the exclusive Bogey Golf Club area, of St. Louis, Missouri, where Addy Michaels was in the living room, playing with her two-year-old son, Robbie. The boy was playing with a toy car that made a sound as he rolled it across the coffee table.

Addy picked up the toy and rolled it over to him. "Roll it back, Robbie," she told him, and he did.

Her husband, Rob Michaels, came down the stairs into the room. "I have to get to the office, Addy," he told her. "What have you got going on today?"

"I have an interview at the Little Flower, Catholic

School. Mary is going to watch Robbie while I'm gone."

"We've been through this a dozen times, Addy," he said, "I don't want you working."

"I want to teach, Rob. I have a degree in education, and I feel useless not working in my field."

"We'll talk about it again tonight, Addy, I have to go."

A short, heavy-set woman came into the room with the vacuum cleaner. "Mrs. Michaels, I need to vacuum now," she said.

"Mary, how many times do I have to tell you? You don't have to be so formal, call me Addy."

"But the mister tells me to do it, Miss Addy."

"Okay, Mary, I'll talk to him about it. You're old enough to be my mother, for goodness sake."

After Addy graduated in 1992, she and Rob lived in his apartment until he finished law school. Their marriage had been almost idyllic. There was rarely a cross word between them. She became pregnant and gave birth to a baby boy, in 1993. They named the boy after his father and called him Robbie. Rob was overjoyed at having a son and was as perfect a husband as Addy could have imagined. He took her out to dinner on a regular basis and bought her anything she wanted. Their lovemaking was almost surreal, Addy thought, and it just could not get any better. She's was happy, truly happy.

When Rob passed the bar, his father made a place for him at his firm and bought them a house in a very exclusive, and expensive, neighborhood in St. Louis.

"Dear God," Addy exclaimed, when she first saw the house, "this makes our house in New Roads look like a mobile home."

"I wanted the best for you, baby," Rob told her. "My dad is a more pretentious man than I am, and he got the house in a deal, according to him."

"But it's our house, isn't it?" she asked him.

"Yes, of course, it's ours. Do you think you'll be happy here?"

"I'll be happy wherever you are, darling." she said, "It's just so big."

"We'll fill it up with kids, baby," he said. "I'll hire you a maid to do the cleaning and to help with the baby."

"I don't really need a maid, but when I go to work, I will need help with Robbie."

"I don't think it's a good idea that you get a job."

"Why not?" she said.

"Dad thinks it doesn't look good for the wife of lawyer in a prestigious law firm to be a common working person.

"Are you serious? A school teacher is not what I would call a common working person. It's not like I'm going to be working in a Seven-Eleven."

"Still, Addy, we would like for you to get involved in community affairs. My mother is director of several community action committees, and it would be good if you would jump in and help her out."

"Well, okay, whatever you think is best. I just had planned to be a school teacher before I ever went to college. It's really what I want to do with my life, other than be married to you and have our babies, I mean."

"Your primary job is to make me, and the family, look good. When we go to functions, conventions, or a party, things like that, you go as my wife, the prettiest woman there."

"Do you have any idea how shallow that sounds?"

"It's not, really, Addy, we're a team. It's all about selling the firm, Michaels, Kennecott, Darbin, and Michaels. We're going to be rich, baby, but we have to play the game."

"I just want to be happy, Rob, and I don't need to be rich to be happy. You and Robbie, and any others that come along, are all I need."

"I understand that, and I feel the same way, but I have to do my part to make my dad's firm successful. I don't get a free ride just because I'm his son."

ⱭⱭⱭ

"Tuco!" Frankie Ross said to his lead man, Bobby Soutullo (So-too-yo), "can you come into my office for a minute?"

The man walked into Frankie's office and sat down. "What's up, boss?" he asked.

"We've got a job in Red Stick," Frankie told him,

"an apartment project, three-hundred units. I'm going to need you to ramrod it for me. It'll be at least a year-long project."

"That's good news, Frankie," Tuco responded, "our biggest job yet."

"I'm going to buy an extended-cab pickup with a back seat and side bins for tools. The vans are not safe to carry three extra men in the back."

"We'll have to start out early."

"I figure if you start out at six, you'll get to the job by seven. I'll pay you travel time, both ways, and I'll spend the first week with you to help get it laid out."

"I won't screw around, boss, I'll get to the job as fast as I can."

"I know you will, Bobby, that's why I asked you to run the job. You'll have Eddie Bergeron, Wallace, Bill, and Tollie, for the duration, unless the job slows down a lot. I may pull Wallace off to help with the service calls, as soon as I can hire a couple of extra people."

"Wallace's brother is looking for a job. He's a good kid, no experience, a couple of years younger than Wallace."

"I'll talk to him. What's his name?"

Billy Theriot. I think he's about eighteen, strong kid."

"Maybe you can train him on this project. I'll leave Wallace with you, and maybe take Bill Packer for service."

"I'll tell Wallace to have Billy give you a call."

"Thanks, Bobby," Frankie said.

c/ɔc/ɔ

Sarah Ross was watching the paving crew putting the finishing touches on the parking lot for her Riverbend fishing camp. They had a machine, with a man on it and a large roller on the front, driving around and around, all over the lot. The asphalt was still hot, and smoke was rising up from the surface.

"It's a multi-quip one-ton R-Two-Thousand-H, asphalt roller," a voice from behind was telling her. She turned to see who the voice belonged to, and Clay Conner was standing there.

"Clay," she said, surprised. "I didn't see you come up behind me."

"I hope I didn't startle you,"

"No, it's okay. What's up?"

"I was passing by and I saw a beautiful woman in coveralls. I said to myself, there is only one woman in Point Coupee Parish that beautiful, so I stopped to see how your new venture is going."

"It's going well, Clay," she said, "I'm breaking new ground here, figuratively and literally." She pointed at the parking lot.

"So, do you have time to show me the layout?"

"Sure, come on," she said. They walked over to the water's edge. "The bait and fishing equipment shop, and the café, will be here, see the stakes, there. The shop will be about nine-hundred square feet, not very large. The café is going to specialize in fancy sandwiches—deli-sandwiches and Po-boys too, of course, oyster, shrimp, roast beef, and such. It will have about ten tables and a counter."

"So, you'll need a couple of cooks and a waitress or two."

"I have a couple of women lined up to wait tables. I just have to find me some cooks, but I've got time yet. The dock and boat house will go right over there," she said, pointing again. "I'm going to have spaces for six, maybe eight bass boats for rentals. I'm going to have a boat launch next to the dock."

"Well, it looks like you've got it all together. I'm impressed with what you've done, not surprised, impressed. You've done your homework, it seems."

"I'm thinking of building me a small house on the other side of the café."

"Will you have dinner with me, Sarah?" he asked her. "There's a really nice restaurant in Baton Rouge I used to take Addy to every so often, when she was still at LSU."

'I'd like that, Clay, yes, I will, thank you."

"Friday night, around seven, be okay?"

"Friday at seven is fine," she said, "I'll see you then."

Clay Connor floated at least ten feet off the ground for the entire day. He was beside himself and had to keep telling himself. "It's just dinner, Clay, calm down. She won't be shopping for a wedding gown on Saturday morning." He was acting like a teenage boy who just asked the head cheerleader to go to the prom with him, and the cheerleader said yes.

He arrived at her house, right at seven o'clock, Friday evening. Sarah was wearing a blue "side ruffle" dress, that came down to her knees, with three-fourth length sleeves. Her hair was down and fell to her shoulders."

"That is a beautiful dress, Sarah," Clay told her, "at least it's beautiful on you."

"I haven't worn it in a very long time. I'm surprised I can still get into it. I've been saving it for a special occasion."

"Well, it's the most special occasion I've had in a very long time, so thank you for wearing it."

Sarah turned men's heads when she and Clay walked into Chalet Brandt. She was forty-three years old and still looked like something that had just stepped out of a sailor's dream. Clay was feeling full of himself just being with her.

He ordered a bottle of wine and they ordered dinner.

"This is the place I was telling you about," Clay said.

"It's really nice," she said.

"I miss having Adeline here. It was wonderful having my daughter around, as much as she was when she was in school. Now she's in St. Louise and I've only seen her once since she left home."

"How is she doing?" Sarah asked.

"Okay, I guess. She has a two-year-old boy she adores. She wanted to teach school, but her husband doesn't want her to work. I think that bummed her out for a while. But I guess she got over it."

"Her son is about the same age as Frankie's girl, Penny."

"Robbie is a good-looking boy, it's been almost a year since I've been to St. Louis to see him and Adeline, but she sends me pictures every so often."

"I guess I'm lucky, my son is still in the town he grew up in, and I imagine he'll never leave."

"I am really sorry about how things worked out, Sarah."

"I know you are, and it's not your fault."

"It broke my heart when Adeline told me. I think a lot of Frankie, he's a good man, one of the best I've ever met."

"I don't think he'll ever get over Addy, excuse me, Adeline," she said. "I should call her Adeline when I'm with you, since you call her that."

"It's not necessary. I thought about calling her Addy since everyone else does. But I just can't seem to do it."

"She was the love of Frankie's life, probably still is. But he's coping. He's insane over his daughter."

"I can relate," Clay said. "I have three of them, but they don't belong to me anymore."

"They never do belong to us for very long. One day, you're changing their diapers and the next day, they're heading down the aisle with somebody else's kid."

Clay just nodded in agreement.

He drove her home, pulled into her driveway, and turned off the engine. Turning toward her, he said, "I can't tell you how nice it was just to be with you tonight."

"I enjoyed it too, Clay, thank you for taking me to dinner, it was very nice."

"I'd love to do it again sometime," he said. He was starting to open his door, to go around and open hers, when she touched his arm.

"Do you want to kiss me, Clay?" she asked him.

Clay looked stunned for a moment. "I've been wanting to kiss you for half my life, Sarah," he said.

She slid closer to him, and he put his arm around her. He drew her closer to him, gently, not roughly or ham-handed, and placed his lips on hers. He kissed her softly, not pressing her. The touch and taste, of her lips was intoxicating to him. She responded, kissing him back with passion. After a few minutes, she pulled away."

"I'm not ready for the he-she thing, just yet, Clay."

"I know, Sarah, I'm not pushing you, believe me, I'm not expecting anything from you that you're not ready for. The kiss was enough. It was more than enough. If you will just consider marrying me, I promise you I'll be good to you and love you the rest of my life."

"When I'm ready to do that, I will come and tell you, Clay. I wouldn't consider ever marrying anyone else."

"You can't imagine how that makes me feel, Sarah, that's just what I needed right now."

The boat launch and the dock were complete. The boat house was almost finished, and the slab for the café, was poured. As Clay passed the location every morning, he made mental notes of the progress. The framing was going up on the bait and fishing supplies shop, and the café was being laid out.

When those two buildings were complete, he noticed, with much joy, that Sarah had not started construction on the house she had talked about.

She had taken him back, in his mind, twenty-five years to a time when he believed it was possible to be happy and content in one's life. He pondered, philosophically, the influence a woman could have on a man. She could give him hope, blissful hope, of a future filled with happiness, a loving wife and children, and the strength to take on the world.

Then, in the course of a day, with a word or an act, she could burn it all down. If a man, any man, thought about it, seriously thought about, the power a woman he loved had over him to make him great or destroy him, that man would burst out laughing when he heard them called, the weaker sex.

In the meantime, Frankie Ross had embarked on the biggest financial gamble of his life. He had stretched his line of credit at the bank perilously thin. The contract on the project in Baton Rouge was just south of a half-million dollars.

He was elated that he'd been able to get a line of credit to buy material and to cover start-up expenses. Frankie was still unaware that Clay Connor had become a de facto silent partner in his business.

"I don't ever want him to know, Martin," Clay told his banker. "If Frankie knows I'm guaranteeing his credit line, it might make him doubt his own ability. He needs to know that he did it all on his own."

"I understand, Clay," Martin said, "but what if he fails, this is a risky project he's taking on. You'd have to tell him then."

"I'll cross that proverbial bridge when I get to it," Clay said, "Frankie won't fail."

"I hope you're right, Clay. I don't know much about the general contractor who's doing the job."

"Southland Builders is a reputable company. I don't anticipate any problems Frankie will have with them."

"I've never even heard of Southland Builders," Martin said, "I assume you have."

"I own the company," Clay said.

"Oh. Okay, I was not aware of that. Should I also assume you'd prefer to keep that between you and me?"

"I would prefer that, yes, Martin."

"I'll keep you informed."

The project was a ten-building complex of medium to higher priced apartments, a clubhouse and pool, and covered parking spaces, one space per unit. A rented storage trailer held material for the job and equipment, such as ladders, drills, and electric saws.

The first task that had to be performed, before any of the work on the buildings could begin, was the installation of temporary power poles at various locations around the jobsite. The poles consisted of an electrical panel, and 120 volts and 240 volts receptacles for drills, saws, and other purposes. Inevitably, there were radios playing in every building, sometimes two or three in close proximity each other. The radios could be a source of distraction and annoyance to some workers on the job. Bobby Soutullo, who went by Tuco, hated radios on a job. They were especially troublesome to the electricians, who had to communicate with each other, when pulling service feeders the length of a building.

Tuco hated roofers almost as much as he hated plumbers. The roofers would come to the job with huge speakers, which they placed on the tops of their vehicles, and turn up the volume, to the highest level possible, so they could hear the music on top of a three-story building. For the men working near the speakers on the ground, it could be maddening. Loud arguments, and even fights, would sometimes break out over the loud music.

On one occasion, when the roofers' music was distractingly detrimental to their work, Tuco went to the temporary power pole, into which the extension cord, for the offending radios was plugged. He took off the neutral wire, to that particular receptacle, and held it to one of the hot phase terminals. This sent 240-volt power to the radios and burned them up, destroyed them. Then he reattached the wiring, as it had been before, closed up the panel, and went back into the building.

When the inevitable visit came from the roofers inquiring about their radios, Tuco shrugged. "I don't know, pal, we've been having some spikes lately. I had a drill blow up last week."

This brought quiet and comfort for about a week, until the radios could be replaced, then the music would begin again. Generally speaking, workers on the job tolerated the annoyance. More often than not, the annoyance with radios playing on a construction site was due more to a difference of opinion over the type music being played. Bill Packer liked country, which Wallace Theriot couldn't stand. Wallace liked rock and roll, which Bill was not fond of. And so, it went, until the buildings were closed in, the individual units sheet-rocked, and the roofing completed.

When the first five buildings were complete and the

landscaping in place around them, the complex management people began renting them out. That part of the project was then blocked to construction traffic. The pool and clubhouse construction began, and, as soon as the pool was opened, tenants from the rented units began using it. It was at this time that Frankie paid his regular weekly visit to the jobsite. He saw the pool and not a small number of women in shorts or swimsuits.

"How do you propose to get the clubhouse wired in the allotted hours, Bobby?" he asked, smiling at his foreman.

"I've thought about that, boss," Tuco replied. "I can't blindfold them, and I can't go ask the ladies to cover themselves. I guess I'll have to do all the looking, myself and report back to the guys what I saw."

Frankie chuckled. "You've got your work cut out for you."

"I'll get it done, Frankie," Tuco said.

Eventually, the project was completed and, after a forty-five day wait, the builder received final payment from the owner. Frankie received his last draw and his retainage money. After paying for the material, payroll, job expenses, and catching up on his line of credit with the bank, the company made thirty-thousand dollars on the job. He gave Tuco a thousand-dollar bonus and the other men, including those who hadn't worked on the project, two-fifty each.

Frankie Ross decided that he was of sufficient age

that he should drop his baby name, his boyhood name, Frankie, and start going by Frank. It was not difficult for new people who came into his life. He introduced himself as Frank Ross, and that was how people addressed him. For old friends, and most of the residents of New Roads, however, he would always be Frankie Ross. His mother refused to comply with his wish. He was still her baby and she would call him Frankie. He accepted that fact. His employees called him anything he told them to because he was the boss. It had been an awkward thing in the first couple of years after he bought the company. He had worked together with Tuco and several of the others when they all worked for Mike Gaudin. Tuco was instrumental in making the change from Mike to Frankie work smoothly. He was the same age as Frankie, and the potential for friction, jealousy, and hurt feelings was ripe with possibilities.

Tuco immediately took over Frankie's role as lead man and began calling Frankie boss. There was mutual respect between them and two lesser men, in the same situation, could have created a disaster.

The housing project in St. Francisville kicked off again, and Frank asked Tuco to put a crew together, consisting of three men, to wire the houses in the project.

"If we had a damned bridge across the river, we could sure save some time. It's a pain in the ass waiting on the ferry," Tuco complained. But it would be eighteen years before Tuco's wish would come true. The John Frank Audubon Bridge would open in May of 2011.

Bill Packer would run one of the two service vans, Wallace Theriot, Eddie Bergeron, and Tollie Martin, the newest apprentice, would take the other service van and work the housing project. Billy Theriot would be the warehouse guy and general flunky. Billy was good with numbers and math, so Frankie kept open the possibility of training him to be an estimator.

Eddie Bergeron was the only employee of the Cajun men who spoke with a thick accent. Often, Frankie had a hard time understanding the man.

"Whafo dat Bobby, he go by Tuco?" Eddie asked Frank one afternoon."

"What's that, Eddie?" Frank replied.

"Excuse me, bawzman, why do Bobby call hisself Tuco?"

"Oh, well, according to Bobby," Frank said, "when Bobby was a baby, his folks were trying to teach him to say his full name. His rendering of his surname, came out, Tuco. Bobby Soutullo, the three-year-old, became Tuco."

"Well, I be damned," Eddie said," I been waundreeng how da hell he got dat name."

"Well now you know, Eddie," Frank said.

കൃക

The marriage between Louise and Justin was surpris-

ingly successful. Justin Cormier was in love with the
woman, crazy in love. Louise Connor took the Cormier
name and Justin was overjoyed about it. Louise had to
quit the ladies action committee and several other positions she held in the upper-crust society fun and games
go-round. Local folks still had their suspicions about Eve
Cormier's death. It was not that Eve was universally
loved so much as it was Louise's arrogant and grating
mannerisms.

Louise had lost her millionaire husband, but had
flown into the arms, and the bed, of the richest man in
Point Coupee Parish. Justin Cormier's bottom-line was
estimated to be just south of four-million dollars. No one
knew for sure, how much he was worth, because Justin
was known to be into some nefarious entanglements, in
addition to his import/export business. It was commonly
believed that the man was running drugs from Central
and South America into Louisiana and points beyond.
Nothing was ever proven, so Justin remained a solid citi-
zen with a brand-new wife. Cormier had his brain caught
in his zipper, as the popular joke went. He took his new
wife into his confidence, showing her every aspect of his
business and his other assets. In a year, she practically
knew as much about running the operation as he did. He
showed her a floor safe that held "enough hundred-dollar
bills to start a fire under a wet elephant." This was Justin's description on the safe's contents.

"There's close to five-hundred grand in this safe," he told her. "This is our parachute, baby."

"What's parachute mean, Justin?" she asked him.

"If we ever have to get out of the country, this is how we bail out."

Louise found it all very exciting, not taking her husband's clandestine games with a lot of seriousness. She figured he was just trying to impress her. His work in bed was even more impressive than all the money.

"I don't need the money, Justin," she once told him, "I'll live with you in a trailer house, if you keep loving me like you do."

The man was a dynamo, a sexual anomaly. He was fifty years old and wanted sex with her almost every day. After one three-day stretch, in which they had sex every day, he again got frisky with her on the fourth day.

"You need to slow down, my darling man," she told him. "You're going to have a heart attack, and then where would I be?"

"You would be a very rich widow," he said, "now, please take off your clothes."

Louise contemplated the possibility that she might be able to boff the man to death, but she thought better about it for fear that *she* might have a heart attack before *he* did. She discovered that she actually loved the man. No one had ever treated her with such fawning attention.

She became the perfect wife and homemaker, cooking his meals and always being ready for anything he wanted to do. If he came in late and wanted to go out to dinner, she would dress quickly and humor him. Occasionally, like on a whim, he would want to go to New Orleans, and they would go. She never mentioned that her parents lived in New Orleans. She didn't want to have to explain her divorce to them.

It was all too perfect, Louise often thought. The world seemed to be just sitting around, waiting for her and Justin to show up and tell it what their latest desire happened to be.

Something had to be wrong with the man. This could not last forever, she thought. One day, something was going to happen that would change everything in her world, she feared. Little did she know.

CHAPTER 8

The Second Time Around

Near the end of 1995, the Riverbend facility was finished. Sarah was making her final walkthrough, wearing her coveralls and a flannel shirt with the sleeves rolled up. She was bagging up some trash when she saw Clay's car pull into the property.

"I'm a mess, Clay," she said as she walked toward him. "You may want to keep your distance."

"Nonsense, Sarah," he said. "You're beautiful, even in coveralls and flannel shirt. How is it going?"

"It's done," she said," I've been doing some cleanup." She still had some smudges on her brow from wiping her hair out of her eyes.

"You've got some dirt on your face," Clay told her, "but it looks good on you."

"You're too kind, sir."

"Well, you did it, Sarah, you realized your dream. I can't begin to tell you how great that is."

"It's been a long-time coming," she said, "a lot of hard work and anguish."

"But you did it, that's what matters. I love it, I love what you've done here, I love that you could do this without anyone helping you, I love it all— I love you, Sarah."

She pursed her lips, and her eyes smiled at him. "I love you too, Clay," she told him.

"You do?" he asked, his heart suddenly shifting into high gear.

"Yeah, I do, Clay, I love you."

"I notice that you didn't build that house you were talking about. Did you run out of money, or just change your mind?"

"Well, I got to thinking,"

"Okay."

"That big house of yours must be very lonely—"

"Are you telling me you're ready?" he interrupted her.

"I'm ready, Clay."

He reached for her, and she jumped into his arms, wrapped her legs around his waist, and her arms around his neck, and they kissed—long, deliberately, and with much passion.

"You've made me the happiest man in the world, Sarah. I love you so, I'll always love you…I have always loved you, I—"

Shut up and kiss me, Clay," she said, and he did, again and again.

"I want to get married in time for Christmas," she told him.

"How about tomorrow?" he replied.

"That would be in time for Christmas."

"Actually, I'd like to have a big wedding, if you don't mind. I want to ask my daughters to come. I'd like to have it outside, maybe, at our house."

"I'd love that, too, Clay, that would be wonderful."

"I'm never seen you look so beautiful, Sarah."

"I guess falling in love is good for me," she said, smiling broadly at him. "Do you want to come over to my place, tonight, Clay?"

"More than I want my next breath of air, honey, but, and don't take this the wrong way, I'd like to wait until you're my wife."

"That's perfect, Clay," she said, "that's the most wonderful thing you could say."

Clay called his two older daughters, Marie and Catherine, and told them he was getting married. They said they would come to the wedding, then he called Adeline.

"Hello, darling," he said, when she picked up the phone, "your dad is getting married."

"Sarah said she would marry you? Oh, Daddy, that's wonderful, I'm so happy for you."

"Wait a minute, baby, how did you know it was Sarah?"

"Sarah Ross is the only woman you would ever marry, that was easy, Daddy."

"I guess you have a point, daughter, yes, she's the one. I need you to be here for the wedding."

"Of course, Daddy, I wouldn't miss it, you know that. I'll be there?"

When Addy told Rob, she was going to her father's wedding, she met some resistance.

"This is not really a good time for you to leave," he told her. "We're going through some very intense negotiations, and I don't need you to be away."

"I'm not going to miss my father's wedding, Rob."

"Who is he marrying? I thought he would be burned out on women by now, after your mother."

"He's marrying the woman, he's been in love with since high school, Sarah Ross."

"Ross, that's the mother of the guy you were going to marry, isn't it?"

"Yes, Sarah is Frankie's mother."

"Will he be at the wedding?" he asked her.

"She's his mother, Rob, so, yeah, I imagine Frankie will be at her wedding. Would you be at your mother's wedding, if she were marrying the man who has loved her since they were in high school?"

"Money is the only thing my mother loves, Addy. I probably would not be invited."

"Well, you're invited to my dad's wedding. I would like for you to go with me."

"That's out of the question. I can't leave the office for even a day or two, right now."

"Then Robbie and I will go."

"You're taking my son," he said, as if it were an abnormal thing.

"No, I'm taking our son. What am I supposed to do with him?"

"Can't Mary keep him?"

"I don't want the maid to keep him, Rob. I'm taking him with me."

ℰℐℰℐ

The wedding took place in Clay Connor's back yard near the boat house. Sarah wore the same blue dress she wore when Clay had taken her out to dinner, on the night he kissed her for the first time in over twenty-five years. She hugged Addy, lovingly, and her two sisters, whom Sarah barely knew. There were easily a hundred guests, townspeople, Frankie Ross's friends, some people neither, Clay nor Sarah, even knew.

The wedding was to be performed by an Irish priest, from the local diocese, a man named Kellen Murphy. Father Murphy wasn't an American of Irish descent. He was an Irishman from the small town of Wexford, in south-west Ireland. Wexford was just across the Saint George's Channel from Wales on the Irish Sea. Father Murphy spoke with a thick Irish brogue, and some of the attendees had a hard time understanding him.

Murphy was almost iconic in Point Coupee and the surrounding Parishes, very well-liked and respected by Catholics and Protestants alike.

"Air yew a Catlick, Frankie boy?" he asked after being introduced to the son of the bride.

"A Catholic? No, sir, Father, not really, I'm not sure exactly what I am. I just try to keep my eyes on Jesus and off the crap in this world."

"Well, nau," Murphy said, "it lukes lake yew gaut it all figgered aut."

"I'm going to keep working on it, Father Murphy, thank you."

The attendees were seated in rows of metal folding chairs that Clay had rented from a store in Baton Rouge. He'd had the good courtesy of renting chairs with padded seats. Everyone appreciated that. Clay had asked Frankie Ross to be his best man, while Sarah had asked Addy to be her maid of honor. The potential problem with that scenario was either not taken into consideration or was ignored.

Frank stood next to Clay, staring at Addy, standing next to his mother. His mind began to drift back to a time when she belonged to him. He'd planned his entire life around Addy Connor, then, all of a sudden, she was gone. A sad, lost, feeling overcame him as he drank in the beauty of her eyes, those brown, almost black eyes that captured his soul and had broken his heart. Suddenly, he realized that those eyes were staring into his, unflinching, not glancing off, or pretending to be looking around the activities going on around them. She was sad, and her eyes showed it, she looked like she was about to cry.

Surely not, he thought. *She's emotional over her father getting married.* It was an emotional event for Frank as well. His mother was getting married. His father had been dead thirteen years. His mother had mourned him all these years, never giving in to temptation or sullying her name or her husband's memory. Sarah Ross had truly fallen in love with Clay Connor, or she wouldn't be marrying him. She hadn't told her son that she was in love with Clay, he just knew. He knew his mother.

The ceremony was beginning. Father Murphy called the four main characters in the event to approach him. "Lydies and gentlemen, this surmony we are abaut to pairform," he began, "is a sacred sacrament of Christ's chairch. We air gathered hair today, in the presence of our Laird, to join together, in holy matrimony, Cly-ton Kaw-nor and Sirah Ross. Who gives this woman to be married?"

"I do," Frank said, "she's my mother.

"Lov is pia-shunt, lov is kaned. It duz naught ane-vy, it duz naught boast, it is naught prow-ud. It duz naught diasowner oh-thers, it is naught self-sia-king, it is naught iasily eye-ngered, it kapes no record of wrongs. Lov duz naught day-light in evil, but ria-joices in the truth. It always protects, always trowsts, always hopes, always pair-severes. Forst Corinthians thirdeen-farr."

In the audience, Bill Packer leaned over to Tuco and ask him, "What the hell does pishunt mean Tuco?

"Patient," Tuco told him.

"I can't understand what the dude is saying. Why does he talk like that?"

"He's Irish, Bill," Tuco said, "that's just his accent."

"He sounds goofy."

"Have you ever talked to Eddie Bergeron for more than ten minutes at one time?"

Bill just nodded his head. "I get your point," he said.

The priest continued, "Cly-ton Kaw-nor, dew yew tyke this woman to be yere wafe?"

"Yes, I do, Father, and I have something to say."

"Give us a moment, Cly-ton, let's see if the gail wonts to marry yew as well."

Sarah started laughing, as did the few, in the crowd, who understood what he said.

"Sirah Ross, do yew tyke this man to be yere hose-bund?"

"I do, Father," she said.

"Okay, Cly-ton, say yere pace."

Clay turned toward Sarah, took her hands in his, and smiled at her. "Sarah, you are the love of my life. I've loved you my entire life, and I know that sounds impossible, but it's not. When I was a kid and I thought about the woman I would eventually marry, it was your face I saw. When I dreamed at night of the perfect woman, she was you. I promise I will love you for the rest of my life." He then turned toward Father Murphy.

"All right," he said, "then by the authority vested in me by the State of Louisiana, and by the grice of almighty Gaud, I pronounce yew hosebund and wafe. Well, don't just stia-nd there, lake a domb bollock, kiss the gail!"

Clay took Sarah in his arms and kissed her. The audience clapped and cheered. Addy hugged Sarah, then her dad, and Frank hugged his mom. He and Addy were standing there, facing each other, while everyone was passing by the newly married couple. "Can I talk to you, Frankie?" she said, "at the boat house."

He followed her to the dock, and they went into the boat house."

"It's really good to see you, Addy," Frank said, "you look well."

"I'm so sorry, Frankie, I'm sorry I hurt you."

"I'm okay," he told her. "I've learned to live with it. Having a daughter has helped me find out who I really am.

There were tears in her eyes, and she looked at him, helplessly. "There is something I have to tell you, Frankie."

"No, Addy, you don't. There is nothing more to say."

"But I still love you, Frankie," she said.

"Aw, hell, Addy, why are you doing this? Was ruining my life not enough?"

She put her arms around his waist, and he embraced her, placing his arms around her and drawing her tight against him. His shirt was soaked with her tears.

"You're married, Addy, *I'm* married." He spoke low, directly into her ear. "We can't do this, it's too late."

Just then, the door to the boat house opened and Hannah walked in. She saw them holding each other and screamed at him. "You liar, you bastard, you told me it was all over for you and her."

"It is over, Hannah," he told her and he let go of Addy. "Go on, Hannah, I'll be along in just a minute. You hurt people, Addy," he said, "I don't think you mean to, but you do. Are you going to hurt your husband, too? I still love you, too, Addy, I always will, but it's too late for us." He walked out of the boat house, but Hannah was gone.

"Is everything okay, Frankie?" Clay asked him after he went into the house for the reception.

"I don't know, Clay," Frankie said, "I just don't know. I am happy, though, that one of us is with the woman he loves."

Marie and Cathryn came into the house and found their father, "We're going to go see Mom, for a few minutes, Daddy, and then go to the airport."

"Where is Adeline, honey?" he asked Marie.

"She said to tell you she loves you and Sarah, very much, but she had to leave. She took Robbie and left to go back home."

Several hours later, the last guest departed the party and left Clay and Sarah alone in the house. Clay was kissing her and telling her again how much he loved her.

"You know something," Sarah said, "I think today is the first time I've ever been in your house. I don't even know where your bedroom is."

"I don't have a bedroom, in this house," he answered.

"What do you mean, where do you sleep?"

"I sleep in our bedroom."

"Oh, I see," she said, "well, you'd better show me where it is. You're not going to get very much sleep tonight."

He picked her up in his arms and carried her up the stairs, with her giggling all the way up. Then he carried her into the bedroom. Laying her down onto the bed, he caught his breath and said, "Damn, I'm glad you're a lightweight. I was afraid, for a moment there, that I wasn't going to make it up those stairs."

The next morning, when Sarah awoke, he was lying there staring at her."

"Good morning," she said, smiling.

"It's the best morning of my life, darling, it's the first morning of the rest of our lives. If you want to keep your name, for your son's sake, or for whatever reason, it's okay with me. I just wanted to let you know that."

"No, I'm yours now," she told him, "I'll be proud to take your name."

"And I am proud to give it to you, thank you, May-sis Kaw-nor," he said, copying Father Murphy. "Now, I only need one more thing from you."

"Okay, what's that?"

"I need you to tell me where you want to go for our honeymoon."

"Oh, wow, I hadn't even considered that. Where do you want to go, Clay?"

"I want to go to the one place you've always wanted to go."

"Ohmygod, Clay, you're such an amazing man, you remembered."

"I never forget anything about you, Sarah. You told me when you were sixteen that you wanted to go to Paris on our honeymoon when we got married. Well, we're married now, and I would love to take you to Paris."

She began crying and had to get a washrag from the bathroom, wet it, and wipe the tears from her eyes. Then she came back to the bed, still crying and wiping her eyes.

"Come on, honey, you don't have to cry. It's just Paris."

"I'm not crying over Paris," she said, "I'm crying because you remembered."

∽∾∽

They flew into Orly Airport and caught the shuttle to the hotel. Le Coeur du Pays was a five-star hotel on Rue Jean Rey in Paris, just a five-minute walk from the Eiffel Tower.

"I'd hope we can get a room high up, so we can see the Eiffel Tower and the city," Clay said.

"I'm sure we can," she said.

Clay went to the front desk, and was fumbling with his reservation receipt, to show the man behind the counter. Sarah was standing beside him. "Let me help you out, darling," she said, and speaking in French, she addressed the desk clerk.

"*Bonjour, nous sommes les Connors, nous avons une réservation.*" she said, explain that they had a reservation.

"Yes, ma'am, I have it here, where are you from?" the man replied, a bit surprised to hear perfect French coming from an American.

"We are from Louisiana, do you have a room with a view?" she asked in French.

"Yes Ma'am, we have a room on the twenty-third floor, for you."

"That will be perfect, thank you, sir."

"Holy cow, baby, I lied to you."

"What do you mean?"

"I told you I remembered everything about you, but I forgot about you being able to speak French."

"My parents spoke Cajun French, all the time I was growing up. I took several years of proper French, starting in junior high."

"I remember that now," he said.

In their room, Sarah was looking out the window at the Eiffel Tower and what she could see of the city. "I can see the Arc de Triomphe," she said.

Clay went over to the window and looked where she was pointing.

"We have to go there, first," he said. "I've seen so many pictures of that place and the street that passes through it. Have you ever seen pictures of the German Army marching through it, stretched out for miles up and down that street?"

"Yes," she said. "The Champs Elysees, the most magnificent street in the world."

"What does that mean?"

"The Champs Elysees means The Elysian Fields," she said.

"The final resting place of the courageous and virtuous, I remember, from Greek Mythology."

"You're right, darling, I am impressed."

"I still remember a few things I learned, in my four years at LSU."

"Are you tired, would you like to take a nap before we go?" she asked him.

"I'm not too tired to take a nap with you."

"I'm looking forward to it, Clay," she said.

They made love and then napped for a couple of hours. When they woke up, they showered and got dressed then left the hotel.

It was a five-minute walk down Rue Jean Rey to Avenue Gustave Eiffel and his famous tower.

"What does Rue Jean Rey, mean, honey?"

"I'm thinking that, Rey, means king, it's king in Spanish, but king, in French, is roi. So, I think Rue Jean Rey, means Jean King Street."

"You think it's named after Billy Jean King?"

"I don't know," Sarah said, "I guess it could be."

Standing on Avenue Gustave Eiffel, looking up at the massive structure, was an awesome experience for the two recently married Americans,

"This is like a dream come true, Clay."

"It really is, baby, I'm glad you talked me into doing this."

"I'm very persuasive, when I want something very badly," she said, laughing.

"Look, there's a pleasant looking little park over there," he said, pointing down the street. "You want to take a walk over there?"

"Okay, let's do it."

A sign on the entrance to the park identified the street as Allee Maurice Baumont. It led into the tree-lined park. "This is beautiful, isn't it, Clay?"

"It's really nice. You want to sit on one of these benches, and just watch the people walk by?"

"Sure," she said. "Do you think anybody will know we are Americans?"

"They'll figure me out, right away, is my guess, but you are much more refined."

"Let's find out, see those folks coming toward us? tell them hello and good afternoon when they get close to us."

"Okay," Clay said, "this sounds like fun." A casually-dressed man and woman approached them.

"Hi, ya'll, how are you doing this nice afternoon?" Clay said, ad-libbing Sarah's script.

"We're doin' great, pal," the man said. "Where you guys from, in the States?

"We're from Louisiana, a small town called New Roads, not far from Baton Rouge. How about you guys?"

"Texas, Dallas," the man responded. "We're celebrating our twenty-fifth wedding anniversary."

"Well, congratulations," Clay said, "we're on our honeymoon."

"No shit?" the man said.

"None whatsoever," Clay told him, "I hope you have a great time on your anniversary."

"Thanks, man, you and your bride do the same."

Clay looked at Sarah, who was sitting there with a sheepish look on her face. He started laughing, hysterically, and she back-handed him across his chest.

"Oh, shut up, smart guy, you should have known they were Americans."

"Me? You're the people expert. Why didn't you know?"

"Let's try again," she said.

The next people to come by were a man and woman with a small child. The man was pushing a baby stroller with a baby girl in it. Sarah assumed the baby was a girl because she was dressed all in pink.

When Clay greeted them, the woman, scowled at him.

"Eat shit and die, you stupid American savage," the woman yelled angrily in French

"He's actually not stupid. He's a millionaire and a lot smarter than you two phonies," Sarah shouted back at her, likewise in French.

"I don't think they're from Texas, honey," Clay said.

"French assholes," Sarah said, fuming.

"What did she say?"

"She invited us over to their house for dinner."

"Really?" Clay said. "Well, it sounded like she didn't really mean it."

Sarah started laughing at that. "I told them we couldn't make it, that's why she got so mad."

"Promise me you'll tell me what really just happened later tonight."

"I promise," she said.

"You have that map, don't you? Where do we go from here?"

"Let's go back to the Eiffel Tower and walk across

the Pont d'lena Bridge to the Trocadero Gardens."

"I'm with you," he said.

Sarah had brought a map and brochures from the hotel that were available to tourists to help them get around in Paris.

"It says here, in the brochure, everything we need to know about the Gardens."

"Read it to me," Clay said. "I love the sound of your voice, especially when you're mad."

"Jardins du Trocadéro—Gardens of the Trocadero—is an open space in Paris, bounded to the northwest by the wings of the Palais de Chaillot and to the southeast by the Seine and the Pont_d'Iéna, with the Eiffel Tower on the opposite bank of the Seine. The main feature, called the Fountain of Warsaw, is a long basin, or water mirror, with twelve fountain creating columns of water twelve meters high, twenty-four smaller fountains four meters high, and ten arches of water.

At one end, facing the Seine, are twenty powerful water cannons, able to project a jet of water fifty meters. Above the long basin are two smaller basins, linked with the lower basin by cascades flanked by thirty-two sprays of water four meters high. These fountains are the only exposition fountains which still exist today and still function as they once did."

"Well. It's a beautiful place, but I'm hungry. You want to get something to eat?"

"I do," she said.

"Let's get something light at the hotel and then go to Jules Verne for dinner tonight."

"That's a very expensive restaurant, Clay," she said.

"Good, I like spending money on you. I finally have a reason to piss away large amounts of cash on someone, and I'm going to take advantage of it."

"I'm not, necessarily, averse to being pampered," she replied.

"That's fortunate, because I don't intend to stop pampering you any time soon"

"Okay, so, dinner tonight, at Jules Verne and the Arc de Triomphe, tomorrow."

"Good plan," Clay said.

Later that evening, they took the elevator up to the second floor of the tower, walked into the restaurant, and Clay handed the maître d' a confirmation slip for their reservation.

The man held up his finger. "Just one moment, sir," he said.

"When did you make reservations?" Sarah asked.

"I made the reservations before we left home," Clay told her.

"My goodness, darling, you think of everything, don't you?"

"I didn't want anything to spoil this, for you."

Clay was wearing his best black suit and a plain red tie. Sarah had gone shopping in Baton Rouge to prepare for Paris. She was wearing a side-ruffle dress, just like the one she wore when Clay first took her out to dinner, except this dress was orange. "You are absolutely stunning," he'd told her, when he first saw her in it."

The maître d returned and led them to a table by the window. Everything was exquisite—the décor, the table settings, the view, everything. Menus were brought, and Clay looked at his, and lay it back down on the table. "It's all in French, you'll have to order for us."

"It's very expensive, Clay," she said.

"I don't want to know," he replied, "Just order whatever we want and don't worry about the price."

"They have five and six course dinners, which should be more than enough for us. Why don't we order the six-course dinner for you, and the five-course dinner for me? They have a choice of either beef or fish. You order the beef, and I'll order the fish, and we can share with each other."

"That is exactly what I was going to recommend, my darling wife."

She chuckled at his effort to make everything so perfect for her. The food came, and they began eating.

"My gosh, Clay, this is really good food, some of the best I've ever had," Sarah said.

"Wait till you taste my grilled catfish," he said, and she burst out laughing. "But you're right, baby, this is some fine food, can't pronounce it, but it eats pretty good."

The bill came and Sarah looked it over, while Clay

watched her and chuckled over the mortified look on her face. "Okay, give me the terrible news," he told her.

"It's five-hundred and forty francs," she said, "I'll tell you how much in dollars, in just a sec." She retrieved a battery-operated calculator from her purse and plugged in some numbers. "That's five-hundred-thirty-five dollars, Clay," she said.

"Hell, Sarah, that's not bad for a meal like this. I'm going to leave Garcon a twenty percent tip, does that sound, about right?"

"That's a good tip, Clay, yes," she said, "That's six-hundred and forty-two dollars. My head is spinning."

"It's only money, sweetie, I'd be just as happy eating a cheeseburger at the New Roads Diner, as long as you were there."

In their room back at the hotel, Clay was coming on-to Sarah, kissing her, tickling her, and rolling around with her on the bed.

"Do you want to see my new negligee I bought for the trip?" she asked him.

"Yes, I would," he said.

She went to the closet, took a box off the shelf and brought it to him. "Here is the box, take a look."

"No, I want to see you in it," he said, "I got pretty worked up today just listening to you speaking French. It's a romance language, you know."

"Would you like for me to speak French when we make love?"

"I'd like that very much, baby," he told her.

She went into the bathroom and came out a few minutes later in her negligee. It was a white see-through, and he could see her panties, through the dressing gown.

"Dear God," he said, "I've died and gone to heaven."

Sarah looked at him, bit her lower lip, and tossed her hair back. Staring at him with a sultry lustful look on her face, she began speaking in French. "They say avocadoes are good for you," she said.

He smiled without taking his eyes off her.

She walked slowly toward him.

"I don't like cabbage and cauliflower."

He took her hand, and gently pulled her onto the bed, rolled her over, and kissed her, like it was the first time. She looked deep into his eyes, and in her sexiest, most inviting voice, she purred to him.

"I love milk and honey, on my lips and tongue."

"I don't have a clue what you said, baby, but I love it."

She took off her negligee, and they made love again. Clay Connor was the happiest man on the planet, he was certain of that fact.

The next day, they called a taxi to pick them up at the hotel. As they were getting into vehicle, she told him to tell the driver where they wanted to go.

"Arc de Triumph," Clay told the driver.

The car pulled out and the man drove across the Pont d'lena bridge and headed onto Avenue du President Wilson. Sarah spoke to the driver in French.

"You're going the wrong way, turn around and take Avenue Pont d'Iena."

The taxi driver looked shocked, but he turned around and did as she told him.

"I'm sorry, ma'am, I got mixed up," he said"

They arrived at the Arc de Triomphe, paid the driver, and got out of the car. They spent the rest of the day walking around on the Champs Elysees. They spent the rest of the week taking a boat ride on the Seine, going to the Louvre, Notre Dame, and other sights of Paris. Every night, they talked for hours about whatever came into their minds, then they made love and slept in each other's arms. Then it was time to go home.

෴

Before Frankie Ross could come to grips with what had happened between him and Addy in the boat house, he had to make things right with his wife. Hannah was distraught, withdrawn, and depressed for weeks after the incident.

"Are you talking to her on the phone, on a regular basis?" Hannah asked him.

"No, Hannah, I'm not. I haven't seen or talked to Addy in four years."

"Then why were you wrapped all around her, in the boat house?"

"I don't know, Hannah. She has some issues in her

life, and she came over and put her arms around me. I was just comforting a friend. There was nothing going on."

"I don't believe you, Frankie," she said.

"I can't change that, Hannah."

After his mother married Clay Connor, Frankie and Hannah moved into Sarah's house on Janis Street, the house he grew up in.

"I'll buy it from you, Mom," he offered but she refused to even consider that possibility.

"It's yours, son, I want you to have it.

Hannah started drinking after the incident in the boat house with Addy. It wasn't noticeable, at first, but before too long, Frankie began to smell it on her breath. He would often come home from work and find her sleeping on the couch while the baby played in her playpen.

He confronted her about it. She promised to quit, but never did. And he was growing more concerned for his daughter than for his marital problems.

Penelope Ross had her mother's hair but she had her father's eyes and complexion. She was a pretty girl, possessing the best features of both parents. Frankie called her Penny Lope, which always seemed to tickle her giggle box. He would say Penny Lope while shaking his head, and the child would giggle. Frankie loved it and often did it for as long as the child would laugh at his facial gyrations and unusual pronunciation of her name. Eventually, however, she would grow tired of the game.

Her laughter would become forced as she tried to continue humoring her father's obvious enjoyment of their own special game.

Frankie began going home during the workday, just to check on Penny and to make sure his wife was not passed out on the couch.

He tried not to think about the incident with Addy. He didn't know what prompted it, but Addy had told him that she still loved him. That haunted him, day and night. He thought about her a lot, and dreamed about her, and about that magical summer they had together, back in 1988.

CHAPTER 9

Of Lawyers and Lunatics

Rob Michaels had earned a reputation in St. Louis, as a very good, young, corporate lawyer. He began to travel in some highly exclusive company. A man named Josh Ingram was the senior attorney for a corporate entity called Ingram and Winkles Enterprises. Ingram met Rob on the golf course near Rob's home and had taken an instant interest in him. Michaels was an up-and-coming lawyer in the St. Louis area and began to get offers from other legal firms.

Rob worked for his father's firm and never thought about leaving. But when some very lucrative offers came his way, he started to reevaluate his importance and the compensation he was receiving in his current job. "I'm getting a lot of job offers, Addy," he told his wife.

"You mean you might leave your father?" she responded.

"I don't know," he said, "the old man and I never got along very well. He's paying me dog-shit."

"But it's a substantial amount of dog-shit, Rob."

He laughed at her whimsical follow up. "I think I can do better, Addy."

"He gave us this house, Rob. I would think that warranted at least some degree of loyalty."

"He didn't give it to us. He let me take over the payments. It will be ours when it's paid for."

"Oh, I thought that seemed too good to be true."

"It was, but don't get me wrong, it's still a very good deal. I just think I should be making more money."

"I can go to work, if we need more money," she said.

"I can't have my wife working. How would that look?"

"I would look like your wife wants to teach school, instead of doing recreational shopping all day long."

"None of the wives of any of the other lawyers in our firm have jobs."

"Maybe they like recreational shopping."

"Let's drop it, Addy. I won't have you working," he said, raising his voice to her.

"But you promised me when we got married that I could teach school if I wanted to."

"I didn't think you were serious," he said. "I thought you were just saying that to get me to marry you."

"To get you to marry me? You asked me to marry you, Rob," she said.

"And why did you marry me, Addy?"

"I married you because I was in love with you."

"Are you still in love with me?"

"Yes, Rob, I am," she said.

"Then do what I ask you to do and forget about teaching school. We don't need the money."

"I don't want to do it for the money," she said, "I want to do it for self-fulfillment and because it's my chosen field."

"I fucking swear, Addy. Do you know how many women would love to be married to me and not have to work?"

"No, I don't know, Rob, why don't you tell me how many?"

"Forget it. I don't have time for this. I have to go to work."

Rob met Josh Ingram and Fred Winkles for lunch the following week. "I am interested in what you do, Josh," he told him. "but how would I fit in, exactly?"

"Your resume is what makes you an asset to our firm. Ingram and Winkles Enterprises manages hundreds of million dollars of construction firm contracts every year.

"What exactly is it you do, Josh?"

Fred Winkles spoke up. "We manage a conglomerate of ten large commercial building contractors, Rob. We help them through the bidding and contract acquisition process. For instance, say, five or six of our companies wish to bid on fifty-million-dollar project. We work with each company to determine which one of the group is most equipped to do the job. Then we arrange the bids to ensure that the selected company gets the contract."

"That sounds like bid-rigging, Fred," Rob said.

"It's really not, Rob. What we do is make sure the customer gets the best possible contractor and finished project possible."

"What do you need me for?"

"You would act as our company attorney and our personal attorney, as well," Josh explained. "All contracts have to be verified by an attorney, to make sure there are no problems with the customer's specs or payment schedules. Also, we have to check the contracts for hidden or vague clauses, such as an accelerated completion schedule and burdensome penalties. That's just a part of it, but that gives you an idea."

"So, what are you offering me?" Rob said.

"Fred brought a printout, showing our total bottom line for last year."

He spread the paperwork out on the table, turning it around so Rob could see it.

"Had you been with us last year, your pre-tax income would have been three million bucks."

Rob was hooked. His father had been paying him three-hundred-thousand a year, plus benefits, and he felt like his old-man was taking advantage of him. He had earned the firm several times that amount.

Now he was becoming bitter about what he believed was mistreatment and not sufficient appreciation of his efforts.

"You may want to talk it over with your wife before you make a final decision, but we'd really like to have you with us, Rob," Josh said.

"My wife is a beautiful woman, Josh, but this would be way over her head. This is my decision. I'll sleep on it and let you know."

"Fair enough, Rob," they both told him. They shook hands and left the restaurant.

Rob told Addy about the opportunity and that he was leaning heavily in that direction.

"You should talk it over with your dad, Rob," she suggested. "This is a big move to make without some advice from someone who has been in the legal business a lot longer than you have."

"If I take their offer, I'll be quitting my dad's company. I doubt he would be very forthcoming with positive advice for me. I'm going to make so much money it will make my dad look like a pauper."

"I never realized you had so much resentment toward you father, Rob."

"My father is only out for himself. These folks are

giving me an opportunity to get super rich. We deserve that," Rob said.

"Have I met the people you are talking about?" Addy asked.

"You've met Josh Ingram, the senior partner, at the golf club."

"Oh, yeah," she said, frowning at him. "That guy is creepy. You better watch out for him. Something about him is just not right."

"So, now you're a psychic? Do you read tea leaves, too?"

"No, it's just a feeling I have."

ထာထာ

In Lafayette, Louisiana, two men were captured by police after robbing a convenience store. Larry Moran and Beau Woodley were booked into the Lafayette Jail. DNA samples were taken from them and entered into the National Crime Database. A match was found to Larry Moran. His DNA matched that of a sample found on a murdered woman from New Roads, Louisiana, one Eve Cormier. Cormier's body had been discovered, in the trunk of her car, which had been driven into Bayou Courtableau off of Highway 190 back in '93. The information available stated that the lead investigator on the case had been a detective named Captain Will Harmon with the State Police. The Lafayette Police notified Captain Harmon, and he came to Lafayette to interview the suspect with the DNA match.

Larry Moran was brought to an interrogation room and cuffed to the table.

Captain Harmon entered the room and sat down across the table from him. "Your arrest record says that you are from New Roads, Larry, is that correct?"

"Yeah, that's right," the man said.

"You ever robbed any convenience stores before?"

"Nope, I just ain't had much work lately, and I got desperate for money. This was my first offense."

"What kind of work do you do?" Harmon asked him.

"Mostly just general labor. I'm a pretty good mechanic but I ain't worked at that full-time in a while."

"You ever killed anybody, Larry?

"What?" the man yelled. "Hell no, I never killed nobody. What kind of bullshit, you tryin' to run at me?"

"Just asking questions, Larry. I checked with the authorities in New Roads, and they told me you used to work for a man named Justin Cormier, is that true?"

"Yeah, I used to drive a delivery truck for him. I'd pick up stuff in New Orleans and deliver it to different places—Atlanta, Dallas, and other towns."

"Did you ever deliver drugs for Mister Cormier?"

"No," Moran said, shaking his head. "Justin bought shit from all over the world and sold it to stores that deal in that kind of stuff."

"He was suspected of drug trafficking and money

laundering. You wouldn't know anything about that, would you?"

"I told you I never delivered any drugs, and I sure as hell ain't never put no money in the laundry."

"Do you recall that Mister Cormier's wife disappeared, back in 1993?"

"I heard that, but I wasn't workin' for him then."

"Mrs. Cormier was murdered, did you know that?"

"I don't read the papers much," Moran said. He gave Captain Harmon a goofy smile, as if he had just cracked a joke."

"Are you familiar with the Bayou Courtableau area, Larry?"

The man just shook his head, but Harmon detected a slight bit of nervousness in the man.

Moran began to fidget.

"So, is that a, no?"

"I don't know nuthin about that," he said. "What else you got?"

"I've got your DNA evidence under Eve Cormier's fingernails, that's what I have," the captain told him. "You care to tell me how that happened?"

"You ain't got shit on me. You're tryin' to railroad me."

"I have enough to indict you, Larry, and I intend to do that. Now, I can save you from the needle if you cooperate with me."

"What do you mean?" Moran said.

"I mean that I think Justin Cormier paid you and your buddy, Woodley, to murder his wife. If you confirm that with me, I'll see that you get a jail sentence instead of the death penalty."

"I think I should probably get a lawyer," Moran said.

"That's fine, Larry, I'll notify the district attorney that's the way you want to go. I see a gurney in your future."

Harmon called the New Roads Police and asked them to pick up Justin Cormier and hold him for questioning.

෧෨෧

Rob Michaels decided to accept Josh Ingram's job offer, despite his father's claim that the Ingram and Winkles were crooked.

"You're going to get your ass in a crack, son," his father told him. "If you get involved with those two shitheads, I mean."

Rob was adamant, however, and he left the firm. Michaels, Kennecott, Darbin, and Michaels would drop the younger Michaels from their name. Dan Michaels had never legally added his son's name to the company's list of partners.

The Ingram-Winkles group was manipulating the bid process on large commercial projects and on multi-family housing projects. Rob Michaels knew that what they were doing was illegal. But after he received over a million dollars from the operation in his first six months with the company, his sense of fair play and his reasoning skills fell by the wayside. He concluded that he could continue for a while and amass a huge sum of money then walk away. He was just the lawyer, he told himself. He didn't have anything to do with the actual juggling of project contract assignments. Who got this job or that job and how the dollar amounts were being manipulated and inflated to provide enormous profits for the jugglers was out of his purview.

When his wife questioned him about the money he was making, he tried to deflect her. "It's just business, Addy, you can't possibly understand how these things work."

"I don't think you can go from making three-hundred-thousand dollars a year to a million dollars in six months without doing something wrong."

"These projects, once they are completed, produce millions and millions of dollars for the owners. There is nothing wrong with padding the bill a little bit, going in, so construction companies can turn a decent profit, stay in business, and continue to provide jobs for common folks."

"You make it sound almost noble," Addy said.

"I'm not saying that, Addy. It's just the way business is done in the construction industry."

Addy Connor Michaels was an unhappy woman. In

the sixth-year of their marriage, she began to lose respect for her husband. She had been so in love with Rob Michaels that she believed he could do no wrong. His contentious relationship with his parents struck Addy as being mostly Rob's fault.

Mona Michaels, Rob's mother, was a superficial and pretentious woman. But she had been genuinely considerate and accepting of Addy as her daughter-in-law and treated her with love and respect. Mona had tried to convince her son that Addy would be happier if he would let her teach school as she had always wanted to do. Rob remained unwavering on the subject, however, and Addy grew more and more frustrated.

Rob's father, Dan, was a gruff and cranky man who didn't seem to like anyone, except perhaps himself. Addy did her best to avoid the man.

Addy decided to do some research on the business in which her husband was engaged. It troubled her greatly that, although her own father was reasonably well off, he had worked hard to earn what he had. But Rob had made a million dollars in only six months for, what appeared to Addy, doing very little actual work.

She found information on the Sherman Ant-trust Act and bid-rigging and price-fixing.

Enacted in 1890, the Sherman Act is among our country's most important and enduring pieces of economic legislation. The Sherman Act prohibits any agreement among competitors to fix prices, rig bids, or engage in other anticompetitive activity. Criminal prosecution of Sherman Act violations is the responsibility of the Antitrust Division of the United States Department of Justice.

Most criminal antitrust prosecutions involve price fixing, bid rigging, or market division or allocation schemes. Each of these forms of collusion may be prosecuted criminally if they occurred, at least in part, within the past five years. Proving such a crime does not require us to show that the conspirators entered into a formal written or express agreement. Price fixing, bid rigging, and other collusive agreements can be established either by direct evidence, such as the testimony of a participant, or by circumstantial evidence, such as suspicious bid patterns, travel and expense reports, telephone records, and business diary entries.

Under the law, price-fixing and bid-rigging schemes are per se violations of the Sherman Anti-Trust Act. This means that where such a collusive scheme has been established, it cannot be justified under the law by arguments or evidence that, for example, the agreed-upon prices were reasonable, the agreement was necessary to prevent or eliminate price cutting or ruinous competition, or the conspirators were merely trying to make sure that each got a fair share of the market.

Addy was convinced her husband was breaking the law, but she knew that talking to him about it would be a waste of time. She considered talking to her father-in-law about it but she was afraid of the repercussions of her doing that, so she remained silent.

She wondered what had happened between them. They had been so happy the first three years of their marriage. Rob was like a man on a cloud when the baby came. Robbie had blessed their lives so much. Addy began to understand why her dad had treated his girls like they were made of gold, incapable of any wrongdoing in his eyes. Now she knew what that felt like, but her marriage had somehow lost its magic. Rob had stopped using pet names for her. He no longer called her baby, honey, sweetie, or any of the other terms of endearment he used to call her. Now he only called her by her name.

Addy could not conceive of their breaking up. She had committed herself to being Rob Michaels's wife, and she intended to make good on that commitment. It was her unhappiness that caused the scene, in her dad's boathouse after his wedding to Sarah. She felt bad for her friend, Hannah. It must have hurt her very much, she was thinking. Addy knew she still loved Frankie Ross, but not like she had loved Rob when she and Rob had first met. Her days now were spent worrying about her husband.

⌀⌀⌀

Justin Cormier was sitting in the interrogation room. He was not cuffed and was not considered a flight risk.

Captain Harmon entered the room and sat down. His first question unsettled Cormier.

"Did you kill your wife, Mister Cormier?"

"No, Detective," Justin said. "I thought you had a suspect."

"A bad actor named Larry Moran. He says you paid him to murder Mrs. Cormier."

"He's lying," Cormier said. "You can't believe anything those two pieces of shit say."

"I didn't mention anyone else, Justin, how did you know there was another man involved?"

"Larry Moran and Beau Woodley are joined at the hip. If Moran was in on it, then you can bet your ass Woodley was too."

"What did you do with the ten grand you withdrew from the bank a few days before your wife went missing?"

"I do a lot of cash business, Detective. I travel all over the country, buying stuff I can sell in my outlets in Louisiana."

"The two men are going to be indicted for the murder. It's just a matter of time before the finger-pointing begins, and my guess is that all their fingers are going to be pointing at you, my friend. I've suspected you were involved in this for five years now. I intend to prove that you killed your wife."

"Well, you're spinning your wheels, man," Justin said. But the worried look on his face told Harmon he had hit a nerve.

Justin went home and told Louise about the latest event. "I'm in a world of shit, Louise," he said. "That detective is out to get me."

"If you're innocent, you have nothing to worry about."

"That's a nice sentiment, baby, but innocent people go to jail all the time, especially in Louisiana."

"Well, I know you're innocent, and I believe that detective will find out the truth."

"I hope you're right," he said. "I sure hope you're right."

Captain Harmon began intense interrogations of both Moran and Woodley. He subjected them to a marathon of questioning, verbal abuse, and offering deals. He had others carry on the work while he napped for a couple of hours from time to time.

"I want Justin Cormier, Beau," he said on one occasion. "I know he paid you two idiots to kill his wife. You tell me that and testify to it in court, and I'll do everything I can to help you."

The two men were just stupid enough to believe there was something he could do to lower their sentences. Finally, Woodley broke, first.

"All right, Cap'n," he said, "Cormier gave us five-thousand dollars, each to kill her. I didn't have anything to do with the actual killing. I was riding my motorcycle behind the car. We took her to the bayou and drove the car off the bridge."

"So, it was your intent to kill her all along?"

"Yeah," he said, "she had to go. She was starting to threaten Justin. Goin' by what he told us, his old lady was threatenin' to sue him for a divorce. He didn't want to lose half his money."

"Did he tell you why the lady wanted a divorce?"

"Oh, yeah, it was pretty much common knowledge. Justin was screwin' this other gal, on the side."

Larry Moran corroborated Woodley's account of the events surrounding the death of Eve Cormier.

"Tell me you side of the story, Larry," Harmon asked him.

"Well, we followed the old lady to the Walmart and waited until she came back to the car. Then I put the gun in her face and made her get in on the passenger's side. I started driving to the place we picked out. Beau and his dad used to fish there a lot when Beau was a boy. The lady started to panic, the farther we drove out of town. She started yellin' at me, cursing me out, and crying, all at the same time. She started grabbin' at me, scratched my head and face. It hurt like all hell. She got so riled up that I thought she was goin' to make me wreck the car. I had to shoot her to shut her up."

"Then you stopped and put her in the trunk of the car?"

"That's right, Beau had to help me with that. The old bitch was heavy." Harmon reached across the table and punched Moran in the right side of his face, knocking him out of his chair, onto the floor.

"What the fuck, asshole?" Moran yelled at Harmon, "Why'd you do that?"

"You murdered the woman and then you have the balls to complain because you needed help putting her in the trunk of her car. What kind of human being are you, you piece of garbage?"

Moran just shrugged his shoulders and said nothing.

"I'm going to be in that room when they execute you, Larry," Harmon said. He pointed at his own face and said, "This is the last face you'll see right before they send you to hell."

❧❦❧

Dreams and schemes have the ability to make a man or break him. Rob Michaels's association with Ingram-Winkles Enterprises was a dream come true, he thought. He had made a proverbial boat load full of money, two million dollars in his first year and doubled it his second year. He was like a man who could do no wrong. Everything he touched seemed to turn into money. Pride and self-confidence can be assets to a man. They can evoke in others trust, loyalty, and the belief that the man can do anything, solve any problem, and ensure a positive and profitable outcome to anything to which he sets his mind.

Pride and self-confidence can also make a man arrogant, lead to hubris and conceit, and give him an overinflated sense of his own importance and abilities. Rob Michaels became arrogant and overbearing. He fell under the spell of money and its false perception that possessing it in large quantities made a man impervious to the pitfalls of life that everyone else must encounter and endure.

Rob's fall from grace was preceded by his introduction to an honest business man named Austin Tolar. Tolar owned a real estate company that was planning to build a fifty-million-dollar office complex in St. Louis for an office management holding company. His conflict with Ingram-Winkles arose when Tolar had the audacity to toss out a bid. The bid had been submitted by a contractor chosen by Ingram-Winkles to do the project. Rob Michaels went to visit Tolar at his office. Tolar and his son, Avery, were at the meeting.

After introductions were made, Rob sat down with the two men in the conference room of their company. "I represent a property management company, called Ingram-Winkles Enterprises, Mister Tolar," Rob began. "We need to ask you to reinstate the bid from Hancock Builders that you rejected."

"Why would I do that, Mister Michaels, Hancock was five-million over budget and three-million over my lowest bid."

"Here's why. Can I call you Austin, Mister Tolar?" Tolar nodded his head. "Here's why, Austin, Ingram-

Winkles manages the assignment of contracts for a large percentage of the construction projects in the state. The cost difference, you noted is an amount added to cover that service."

"That sounds like bullshit, Rob. I don't need a company to manage assignment of my contracts. I do that myself."

"The eventual owners of the project bear the brunt of the additional cost, Austin," Rob said.

"But I don't want the owners to bear the brunt of any additional costs," Tolar responded, "I want to build their project for the lowest possible cost."

"The additional cost covers the detrimental effects of slow pay, retainage, and removes the burden incurred by sub-contractors when they have to wait an inordinate amount of time for their draws. Also, we believe that Hancock is better equipped and more capable of doing the job in the time-frame allotted."

"I've worked with Precepts Construction Company before, and they have always delivered a good product, in a timely manner."

"But things happen, Austin, unforeseen delays, bad weather, and union trouble. If Hancock does the job, we can guarantee that these delays will be eliminated."

"Can your company control the weather, Rob?" Tolar asked him, and all three men laughed.

"No, sir, we cannot control the weather, but we can control most of the other possibilities I mentioned."

"Let me think on this for a few days, Mister Michaels, Tolar said, "I'll call you before the weekend."

Austin Tolar was a textbook example of the greatness of the American concept of opportunity for all. That was, for all who are willing to work hard, play by the rules, and treat people with honesty and respect. He did not cheat on his taxes, he paid his employees a fair wage, he didn't cheat his customers, and he never backed down from bullies, which he believed the organization, represented by Rob Michaels to be.

Rob got a call from Tolar on Friday of that week. "Hello, Rob, I told you I'd call you as soon as I made a decision on the Hancock bid," Tolar said.

"Yes, Austin, can we count on you to do business with us?"

"I'm going to stick with Precepts on this, Rob. I just can't make a case for using Hancock."

"Well, that's disappointing, Austin," Rob said, "I was hoping for a more positive outcome, but I'll let them know."

"Do you mind if I give you some advice, Rob?"

"No, sir, not at all," he said.

"You seem like a nice young man. You should get away from Josh Ingram just as fast as you can. Start your own practice or join another legal firm, anything but staying involved with that bunch. They're not honest people."

"I'll take that under consideration, Austin, thank you."

When Rob got home that evening, he asked his wife to come to the living room after she had put Robbie to sleep.

"He's sleeping now," Addy said, as she sat down on the couch beside him. What's up?"

"I think I'm going to leave Ingram-Winkles and find another job or start my own firm."

"Oh, thank goodness. I was so hoping you would decide to do that, Rob. Are you going to tell your dad?"

"I don't know, yet," he said, "I'll have to eventually. But I think I'll wait a while. I'm not ready to hear, 'I told you so' from my old man."

In the ensuing weeks after the project had started, the jobsite experienced a couple of break-ins and some stolen property. The superintendent's trailer was set on fire and tires were slashed on the backhoes and forklifts.

Austin Tolar called Rob again about the vandalism.

"I took your advice, Austin, and ended my association with Josh Ingram. I honestly don't know anything about what they might be doing, now. If you think it will help, I'll call Josh and talk to him about it."

"No, that's okay, Rob, Josh Ingram is certainly not going to admit to being involved in this mayhem, and he's not going to stop. I'll handle it myself."

Rob found it interesting that Tolar said he would handle the problem himself. It seemed like a suspicious response for an honest man. He wondered what the man had in mind.

About a month later, Rob found out, what Austin To-lar had in mind when FBI agents came to his door and placed him under arrest. "What am I being charged with?" he asked them.

The agent in charge told him. "You're being charged with violation of the Sherman Anti-Trust Act, bid-rigging and price-fixing under the RICO Statute, your two part-ners are already being booked, as we speak."

Addy was at the grocery store, so Rob called his mother, told her what was happening, and ask her to call Addy when she got home.

When Addy got home, Rob's mother, Mona, was parked in the driveway. She told her what had happened and advised her to go back home to Louisiana for a while.

"This is not going to blow over," Mona told her, "You don't want to be here with all this going on."

"But I can't leave my husband, when he needs me the most."

"He doesn't need you now, Addy, and you don't want Robbie exposed to all this mess. They don't suspect you of any wrongdoing, and you won't need to testify on Rob's behalf."

Addy would not leave before she knew what was go-ing to happen to Rob. She stayed and went about her business like nothing was wrong and everything was go-ing to be all right.

At the trial, Rob discovered that Austin Tolar had been cooperating with the government, to take down Ingram-Winkles Enterprises for the same crimes with which he had been charged. Rob argued that he was only the attorney for the company and had nothing to do with the actual management of the business. It would have worked had not Rob gone to meet with Austin Tolar and his son Avery. Their conversation had been recorded, and both men testified that the voice on the recorder was indeed, that of Rob Michaels.

The Ingram-Winkles Corporation was fined the maximum amount allowed by law, ten million dollars, and each man, including Rob Michaels, received a sentence of five-years in prison. Michaels was fined the maximum, three hundred fifty thousand-dollars. He was also assessed an additional fine of two-million-dollars, for damages incurred by owners of various construction projects, he and Ingram-Winkles had bilked in their illegal activities.

Addy was heartbroken and confused. Her father-in-law came to the house to talk to her. He was surprisingly congenial.

"Sit down, Addy," Dan Michaels said.

She did as he asked.

"I'm really sorry, honey, for what my son put you through. I know you tried to talk him out of going in with Josh Ingram. He told his mother you did, and she told me. Rob doesn't deserve a woman like you."

"What is going to happen, now, Mister, Michaels?" she asked.

"Please, Addy, call me Dan. I haven't been very nice to you since he married you and brought you home. I apologize for that. I realize now what a quality person you really are."

"I'll wait for him until he gets out," she said.

"No, I don't want you to do that. I know you want to teach school. I tried to get Rob to let you do that, but he had some cockamamy idea that it wasn't appropriate. It's my regret that I wasn't more influential with him on that. You need to file for divorce, and I will handle all that for you."

"But I don't want a divorce. I love Rob," she said.

"I know you do, Addy, but we need to remove any and all suspicion that you might have known what Rob was doing and didn't say anything about it. The best way to accomplish that is to divorce him. You have to trust me on this."

"Okay, Dan, I trust you," she said. "What do I do now?"

"First, we're going to get you a new car, and you're going to pack up everything you have to have to get started back in Louisiana. I'll have everything you own packed up and shipped to you as soon as you give me an address. I have your cell phone number and email address, so we can communicate."

"It's all so unreal," she said, almost in a stupor.

"This house is yours, Addy, but I'm going to sell it and send you the money. You'll owe some taxes on the earnings, so don't spend it all in one place."

She chuckled. "I'm trying to process all this, I'm going to call my daddy later and let him know."

"The only thing I ask of you, Addy, is that you stay in touch and let us visit our grandson as often as possible. You are our daughter-in-law, and we do love you, no matter how much it may appear to the contrary."

"Oh, of course, Dan. You can see Robbie whenever you want to. I'll bring him here in the summer between school years. Thank you for all you're doing for me."

"It's the least I can do, Addy, for everything my son did to you and his son."

Later that night, Addy called her father in New Roads.

"Hello, darling," Clay said, when he saw his daughter's number on his phone window,

"Daddy," she said, "I'm coming home."

CHAPTER 10

Hearts in Default

Justin Cormier kissed his wife goodbye and headed out the door.

"Will you be late?" Louise asked him.

"A little, maybe," he responded. "I have to go to New Orleans."

When he didn't come home that evening, Louise called his cell phone, but he didn't answer. She began to worry that something might have happened to him. She called the local police station.

"Relax, Louise," the chief told her, "Eve was always reporting him missing. He'll turn up, believe me."

But Justin didn't turn up. After a week, and still no

Justin, the New Roads Police put out an APB on the man and notified Captain Harmon of the state police.

"I hope that sonofabitch hasn't skipped out on us," Harmon told the chief.

"I do too, Will," the chief said.

Captain Harmon called Louise Cormier and asked her if he could come to the house and talk to her. She agreed and he drove to New Roads the next day.

"How was your husband's demeanor, the last time you saw him?"

"I didn't notice anything different about him, Detective. He said he had to go to New Orleans. The only strange thing about that morning…"

"Yes, ma'am?" Harmon said.

"He didn't have sex with me that morning."

"I see," he replied. "Now, I'm going to ask you a question, and I hope you don't take this as just my curiosity—"

"Yes, Captain Harmon," she interrupted, "we have sex every morning—every night and every morning."

"I was just trying to get an idea what his state of mind was. If he broke a routine, it could indicate that he was preoccupied or might have been planning something, you know, like skipping out."

"I don't know. I didn't get the impression that he was that way, but then it was very early."

"What time did he leave, that morning?"

"It was around six," Louise said.

"Did your husband have a stash of money, that you know of?"

"I don't know," she said. "He has a floor safe, but I don't know what's in it."

"Do you have the combination?"

"No, I don't. Justin had it written on the back of one of his business cards. I can get it for you."

"If you don't mind, I'd like to take a look. If he took a stash of money that morning, it could mean he was intending to flee the state."

The safe was empty, except for important papers, the house title, and other miscellaneous documents. Harmon was stumped. "Do you know if your husband kept any money in this safe, Mrs. Cormier?"

"I never saw him put any money in it or take any out," she told him.

Harmon went to the police station to talk to the chief. "Didn't you tell me that Justin Cormier has a fishing cabin somewhere on the lake?"

"Yes, on the other side of the lake."

"Have you gone to check on it? He could be holed up there."

"Somebody would have seen him, Captain. He couldn't stay there very long without some neighbor or someone spotting him. And with his face all over the TV, somebody would have called, don't you think?"

"I suppose you're right," Harmon said.

Justin Cormier would remain missing, for the time being.

ฅ๑ฅ๑

Frank Ross was chasing his daughter down the street. He'd bought her a battery-operated car, and she had become proficient in maneuvering the toy vehicle around trees and other yard items. She was instructed not to drive it in the street but she often forgot that rule, so her father had to run her down and direct her back to the side of the road.

Penelope, called Penny Lope, was the light of her father's life. The lovely little, brown-haired, brown-eyed sprite was indeed her father's daughter.

"Come on Penny Lope, race Daddy to the corner."

The girl lowered her head and drove the little car toward the end of the street, as fast as it would go.

"Run, Daddy," she yelled as Frankie caught up to her.

He slowed his pace to let her get to the corner first.

"I win, Daddy, I beat you," she squealed and started giggling happily.

"Good job, baby, I just couldn't keep up with you," he said. "Come on, it's too dangerous in the street, let's go to the park."

"I think you let me win, Daddy," the energetic six-year-old said after they were at the park.

"You do? Now what makes you think I let you win?"

"You slowed down, when you got ahead of me. I think you let me win."

"You're a pretty smart girl, darling." he told her, and she smiled brightly.

They played for about an hour, and then Frank told her they needed to go home and check on Mommy.

It was one o'clock, in the afternoon, and Hannah was still in bed in a drunken stupor. She had started drinking after the incident at Clay and Sarah's wedding and never stopped. Frankie woke her up and made her get dressed.

"We're going to get something to eat," he told her.

"I don't want to go," Hannah replied.

"I'm worried about you, Hannah, and I worry about Penny, when she's with you. You have to snap out of this. It's not healthy for you and it's not good for our daughter to see you like this, all the time"

"I watch her, Frank, I'm a good mother."

"You're always drunk, Hannah. You have to stop drinking."

"Why?" she said. "If I die, you'll be free to marry Addy Connor."

"Aw, hell, Hannah, how many times do we have to go over this?"

"As many times as I want to," she said.

"Well, I'm done with it. If you don't stop this nonsense and stop drinking, I'm going to divorce you."

"Please don't divorce me, Frank, I love you. I can't live without you."

"Then stop drinking, and I won't," he shouted at her.

But Hannah Ross was a victim of her own demons.

She had been best friends with Addy Connor since junior high, and she held a burning hatred for her. Addy was beautiful, and Hannah was plain looking and devoid of personality. Her greatest envy of Addy was that Frankie Ross loved Addy and didn't appear to know that Hannah was even alive. Hannah loved Frankie secretly. She never told anyone until she told him, years later, after Addy had married another man, and Frankie was free. Becoming pregnant had gotten Frankie to marry her. She gloated over it but suspected that he still loved Addy. Her fear was confirmed at the Connor-Ross wedding when she caught Frankie and Addy in each other's arms in the Connors' boat house. Hannah lost her will to live and no amount of reconciliation on the part of her husband could ease her troubled mind.

Captain Harmon got a call, in his Baton Rouge office from the chief of police of New Roads, a man named Steve Guidry.

"Hello, Chief," Harmon said. "Please tell me you've found Justin Cormier."

"We've found him, Will, but you won't like the condition he's in."

"You didn't kill him, did you?"

"Cormier punched his own ticket, Will," the chief said.

"Are you shitting me, Steve?"

"No, Will, I'm not. We got a call from a neighbor of his at his fishing camp. The guy said Justin's car had been parked behind the house for a very long time. I took a couple of my men and we went to check it out. He was on his bed with a bullet hole in his head. His gun was lying on the floor beside him."

"Well, I was looking forward to seeing him go to prison, but I guess justice is served, just the same. A slick lawyer might have gotten him off. The testimony of those two shitheads could have been challenged. Cormier would have claimed they were robbing his wife and killed her when she started fighting back. And he might have been convincing."

"Well, he's got to answer to God, now, and all his money won't help him in that venue."

"Have you told his wife, yet?" Harmon asked.

"I'm going there now, Will. Good luck to you, I'll see you next time there's a need."

"Same to you, Steve, take care of yourself, and thank you for all your help."

Louise was distraught. She broke down, weeping and shaking all over. The chief and his two officers tried to comfort her, but she would not be comforted. They talked her into lying down on the couch. One of them brought her a wet rag which she placed on her head. Then they left her to suffer alone. Louise continued grieving over Justin, all night long. When she awoke, the next morning, a thought came to her mind, and she started laughing hysterically. She suddenly remembered that Justin had changed his will and named Louise as his only beneficiary. She owned it all, the house, the business, the fishing camp, and the five-hundred-thousand-dollars she had taken from the floor safe and hid in the attic in a trash bag. A visit to Justin's accountant, a bookish man named, Roland Fontenot (Fonten-no), informed her that she was now worth just a tad north of four-million-dollars.

"I want you to keep working for me," she told the accountant, who was more than happy to keep his job. "I need to find someone to run the company, for me, can you do that?"

"Let me think on it, Mrs. Cormier," he said, "I'll figure something out."

"Thank you, Roland, and call me Louise, if you don't mind."

When Clay Connor heard the news, of Justin Cormier's death, he chuckled over what that meant for Louise. The woman was now the richest person in Point Coupee, Parish. And possibly the richest for several parishes around. He wondered how long it would take her to piss it all away.

❧❧❧

Hannah Ross was sitting in a lawn chair in the front yard of the Ross home, watching her daughter, Penny Ross, race around the yard in her play car. In Hannah's hand was a drinking glass that contained straight bourbon and several ice cubes. She finished the drink and got up to go into the house to pour another one, leaving Penny unsupervised. After finishing that drink, Hannah started getting drowsy, dropped the glass onto the ground, and fell into unconsciousness. She was awakened by the sound of screeching tires and her daughter screaming.

Penny had driven the little car into the road from in front of a parked car. The driver of the car, on the street did not see her and ran into her, the wheel of his car pushing her about twenty feet before he could come to a stop. Hannah tried to wake up and get out of her chair, but she fell over and lay there in the grass.

The man driving the car ran to the nearest house and asked them to call an ambulance. The EMT arrived very quickly, treated Penny as best they could, while transporting her to the hospital. The police, accompanying the EMT vehicle, knew Frank Ross and called him. Frank dropped what he was doing and went to the hospital right away.

"Hello," he said to the nurse at the information desk, "I'm Frank Ross, my daughter was just brought in, can you tell me where she is?"

"She's in surgery, at the moment, Frank," the nurse told him and directed him where to go. "The doctors are taking care of her now. Someone will let you know her status, just as soon as they can."

Frank sat down on a chair in a small waiting area near the operating room. He lowered his head into his hands and began sobbing. "Oh, God," he said quietly to himself. "I can't lose my baby. She's all I have left." He was still crying when a doctor approached him.

"You're Frank Ross?" the man asked him.

"Yes, sir," Frank said. "How is my daughter?"

"She'll be okay, Frank," the doctor said. "She has some pretty severe injuries, a broken leg, and several pretty serious, bruises. She'll take some time to heal, but she will. I'm Doctor Massey, and I will keep you informed."

"Thank you, Doctor," Frank said. He lowered his head and said, "Thank you, God, for saving my baby."

The police intended to arrest Hannah for child neglect, but after several hours, she had not sobered up enough to even know what was happening to her. They took her to the hospital.

Clay and Sarah came to the hospital, and found Frank sitting in the waiting room. He stood up and they both hugged him. "She's going to be okay, Mom," he said.

"I know, Frank, we talked to the doctor."

"Hey, Clay," Frank said, "thank you for coming. How did you hear about it?"

"The police called, me, Frank. They found Hannah passed out on the lawn, drunk," he told him.

"Oh, hell, I don't know what I'm going to do. Hannah won't stop drinking, and I can't ever leave her with Penny, again."

Chief Guidry found Frank, in the waiting room. "The

paramedics brought Hannah in, just a short while ago, Frank. They couldn't wake her up. She was unresponsive. You may want to call her parents."

"Thank you, Chief," Frank told him. "I'll do that right away."

It was an hour before Lane and Betty Morley got to the hospital. Since he and Hannah had married, the Morleys had moved to Baton Rouge because her father, Lane, had changed jobs. Frank did his best to comfort them.

"I'm sorry, Lane, I would have let you know sooner, but I didn't find out that she was here until just a few minutes before I called you."

"They told us she has alcohol poisoning, Frank. I knew she had started drinking, but I had no idea it was this bad."

"She was passed out in her chair, in the front yard when Penny was hit by a car."

"Oh, dear God," Betty Morley exclaimed. "How is my granddaughter?"

"She's going to be okay, Betty, but she has a broken leg and is bruised pretty bad. They're still working on her."

The woman started crying and was inconsolable. "My baby, and her baby, all at once, I can't accept this," she said, almost out of her mind.

A doctor entered the room and asked them to sit down. "I'm Doctor, Peters, folks, and I want to advise you of your daughter's condition. She was unresponsive when they brought her in. What we have determined is that Hannah had apparently consumed a toxic amount of alcohol in a very short period of time."

"What does toxic mean, Doctor?" Lane Morley asked.

"It means poisonous, Mister Morley. Hannah has alcohol poisoning. She is still passed out and unresponsive. You see, when a person takes in an inordinate amount of alcohol in such a short period of time, as the alcohol continues to pass from the stomach and raise the blood alcohol level in the body, the person's brain gets so drunk that it simply forgets to tell some body functions to continue working. That's pretty much what has happened to Hannah. We are doing everything we can to save her."

Frank left the Morelys and went back to the operating room, where his daughter was being treated. Clay and Sarah were still there, waiting for him.

"How is Hannah?" his mother asked.

"I don't know, Mom, it's pretty serious. Only time will tell."

"The doctor said we can see Penny now. You can go in alone, if you want to."

"No, she'll be happy to see you both, too."

Frank burst into tears when he saw her. Penny's left leg was in a cast and she was bandaged, almost from her head to her toes. He kissed her on her head, but didn't touch the rest of her, for fear of hurting her. "Hi, baby," he said, still crying.

"Hi, Daddy," Penny said, and she looked at Sarah and Clay. "Hi, Grandma, hi, Grandpa, thank you for coming to see me."

Sarah was strong but Clay became emotional over her calling him Grandpa. It was the first time she had called him that, and he was moved to tears.

"Where's Mommy?" Penny asked.

"Mommy is not feeling well, baby," Frank told her. "She'll come to see you when she gets better."

But Hannah did not get better. She never came out of her alcohol-induced coma. Hanna Ross passed away that night, right around midnight. Frank learned about it when he went back to check on the Morleys. They were sitting on the couch in the waiting room, wrapped in each other's arms, weeping uncontrollably. He didn't have to ask, he knew that his wife had died.

෴

Roland Fontenot called Louise and told her he had set up a meeting, at his office for her to meet the man who had been running Justin's company for him. She arrived at Roland's office early, before the man who was to meet her arrived.

"Tell me a little about this man, Roland," she said.

"His name is Morris Hebert."

"Dammit," she exclaimed. "Is every sonofabitch, in this company, a Coon-ass?"

Roland just looked at her.

"I'm sorry, Roland, I didn't mean to demean you, or anyone else. I don't have anything against Cajuns. Hell, I married one. What exactly is a Cajun, anyway?"

"It's okay, Louise," he said, "but, in answer to your question, yes, the population of New Roads is predominantly of Cajun extraction. The term Cajun is a vernacular, so to speak, for the Acadian exiles in Canada. They were French-speaking people from what is now the Maritimes of Eastern Canada. They settled in Louisiana and Acadians morphed into Cajuns."

"I'm sorry, Roland," she said, "and I apologize. This fellow who's coming, do you recommend that I keep him on?"

"I do, Louise. Morris is a good man. He has, basically, run the company for years, in spite of interference from Justin."

Just then, Hebert walked in the door.

"Sorry I'm late, Roland. I had some last-minute paperwork before I could break away."

"No problem, Morris, I understand. Morris, this is Mrs. Cormier, Louise Cormier."

Morris extended his hand and she shook it.

"I'm happy to meet you, ma'am."

"Oh, for goodness sake, call me Louise," she said, and Morris nodded. "How long have you worked for my husband?"

"Right on ten years now, Louise.

"Do you mind if I ask you what kind of man he was—to work for, I mean?"

"No, I don't mind," Morris said. "Justin pretty much left me alone to do my job. He actually didn't come around very often."

"Did you like him, personally, Morris?" she asked. "I'm just asking to find out how to deal with you and the other employees. This is new to me, and I don't want to screw it up."

"Do you want an honest answer, Louise?"

"I would really appreciate it, Morris, if you would always tell me exactly what is on your mind, even if it's something I might not want to hear."

"Fair enough, ma'am," he said. "I will always tell you the truth. I didn't like your husband, personally. I didn't let that interfere with how I did my job. But Justin was shady, in my opinion. It is rumored that he was dealing drugs all over North Luziana. I don't know if that was true, or not, but that was the rumor."

"Do you harbor any resentment toward me for marrying Justin, so relatively soon after his wife's death?"

"None at all, Louise, that didn't affect my job, at all, and your reasons for marrying Justin are your own. He told me you were a beautiful woman, and I see now, that's probably the only time he didn't lie to me about something."

Louise was shocked at what he had said, and she began sizing him up. He was taller than Justin, about six feet, she estimated. He was a good-looking man, and the prematurely graying, around the temples of his coal black hair made him very attractive. She quickly put those thoughts out of her mind and went back to business.

"That's very nice of you to say that, Morris, thank you. Now, do you need anything, a raise or anything else, to continue in your current position?"

"No, Louise, Justin paid me well. I'm okay. I'll do everything I can to make your company successful."

"Thank you, Morris," she said, "If you have any problems, or suggestions, call me personally. Here is my card. It has my cell phone number, too, but, as I'm sure you know, cell phone service in New Roads is pretty shitty."

"Thank you, Louise. I'll keep you apprised of anything I think you should know."

♥ↄ♥ↄ

Hannah was buried in the cemetery on Main Street because she had grown up in New Roads and had rarely ever left it. Lane and Betty Morley thanked Frank for the patience he'd shown toward their daughter.

"I know it's been tough for you the past few years," Lane Morley told him. "You did the best you could. I don't know what else you could have done differently. My daughter was self-destructive."

Frank assured them that they could come and see

their granddaughter any time they wanted and that he would bring her to Baton Rouge to see them, every chance he got.

It was months before Penny was completely healed, and almost a year until she lost the limp in her left leg.

He couldn't stop himself from thinking about Addy. He had tried, with all that was in him, to convince Hannah that he was not still in love with Addy. But it was impossible for him to make her believe it. It was just too big a lie for him to tell and be believable.

Addy was never very far from his mind. He ached to see her again. She invaded his dreams at night. He was thirty-years old, and his only reason for living was his daughter, the only good thing produced from his marriage to Hannah Morley. His hope was that, one day, the only woman he'd ever loved, would somehow come back into his life.

CHAPTER 11

Coming Together

Sarah Connor was a working woman. Her dream had come true, and her business was up and running. The only problem was that Sarah was not comfortable leaving the day-to-day operations to hired hands. She was there every morning like clockwork to open up and to make sure the cooks and waitresses and the fishing supply manager showed up for work.

Clay had bought her one bass boat, and she had bought another one. She decided to keep just the two boats and lease the other six slips for people to keep their boats in. The six slips had been occupied for the last six months.

Riverbend became one of the most popular places on the lake. She took Clay's suggestions on several things he said would help business. One was that she let anyone use the boat launch ramp for free and to leave their vehicles in the parking lot at no charge. It would draw people to the place.

People who launched their boats would, invariably, have a snack in the café and buy something from the fishing supply. Also, according to her husband, the extra vehicles in the parking lot, while not bringing in any cash, would give the perception that the business was very busy, so it must be really good. The validity of that that theory was borne out by the influx of patrons to the café and the other services available to passersby.

Sarah was very personable, a natural, business person. She was very well liked by her customers and employees alike. The older men were especially fond of the friendly, attractive woman. At least one marriage proposal a week was not uncommon for her, along with all the flirting that came her way. Sarah took it in stride. It was good for business and most of them were not serious.

"Sarah," one regular elderly man said to her once, "if you'll just promise me that, when I die, you will come to my funeral and kiss my casket, I will rest easy until the good Lord comes to get me. And be sure to wear a lot of lipstick, I want it to show."

"And you're certain, Wally, that your wife is going to be okay with me kissing around on your casket?"

"Aw, the hell with her, just kiss it and run, Sarah."

"I promise, Wally," she said, laughing at his humor."

Frank was having lunch at the diner in New Roads on one occasion when the man, sitting beside him at the counter, began talking about Riverbend. "It's the best facility of that kind on the lake," he said. "They let you launch your boat for free, the café has some really good food, and the supply store has everything you can possibly need. And that lady who owns the place is so damned good-looking, she almost makes me cry."

Frank was nodding his head.

"You, seen her?" he asked Frank.

"Yeah, I've seen her," Frankie replied. "She's old enough to be my mother, but she's a hottie, all right."

"She ain't that old," the man said. "She looks to be in her late thirties or early forties, maybe. She's a good-looking thing."

"You may be right. I can't say how old she is," Frank told him.

Sarah and Clay got a big laugh out of that when he told them.

One Saturday morning, Clay asked Frank for a favor. "If you don't mind, Frankie, I need you to drive to my condo in BR and pick up a couple of things for me."

"Sure, Clay, I'd be happy to do that,"

"The address is on this note pad. There's a lady there taking care of the place. You can take my car."

He found the address in an upscale condominium

project. He rang the doorbell and the door opened. Frank was struck dumb and could not speak.

"Hello, Frankie," Addy said. "Cat got your tongue?"

"What are you doing her, Addy?" he asked her, still barely able to speak.

"I live here," she said. "Will you come in, I need to talk to you." He walked into the house, and she told him to sit down.

"You're limping, what's wrong?"

"I turned my ankle a couple of days ago. I took off Thursday and Friday, but it hasn't gotten much better."

"Took off?" he said, looking confused.

"I'm teaching school in Baton Rouge," she told him.

"I don't understand, Addy."

"It's a long story. Do you have to go?"

"No, I don't have to go."

"Oh, me, where to start. I'm divorced, Frankie," she said.

"That's a good place to start, Addy," he said. "I guess I don't have to look over my shoulder for a husband to come down the stairs." She laughed at that. "How long have you been here?"

"I've been here almost a year."

"A year, you've been here a year. Why did you not call me, Addy? You know I love you. Why didn't you call me just to let me know you were okay, if for no other reason? Are you trying to break my heart all over again?"

"No, Frankie. I couldn't call you, you were married. My daddy told me I couldn't break up your marriage. I came back home because it's home. I wanted to see you, but I couldn't hurt Hannah and destroy your marriage. I've been dying, literally dying, to see you or just to hear your voice. I've messed up things so badly. I can't imagine why you would still love me."

"Because you're the love of my life, Addy, I told you when you broke up with me that I would always love you, even if you lived happily ever after with another man. Everything in my life has just been marking time until you came back to me."

"If you still want to marry me, Frankie, will you let me teach school? I love teaching school."

"What kind of question is that?" he said. "Of course, I'll let you teach school. What kind of man wouldn't want his wife doing something she loves?"

"The kind I married," she said, choking back tears.

"Really?"

"After we moved to St. Louis, Rob became self-centered and arrogant. He refused to let me pursue my teaching career, said it wasn't befitting a man of his stature." She got up from the couch. "Would you like some coffee?"

"Sure," Frank said.

Addy stumbled, her ankle gave out, and he caught her arm and steadied her.

"Sit down, let me look at your ankle." He took her foot in his hands and began massaging it. "Does that hurt?"

"A little but it feels good, don't stop."

He continued massaging the foot and ankle. Then he took her pinky toe between his index finger and thumb and rubbed the underside of the toe.

Addy let out a yelp and started giggling.

"Ohmygod, Frankie, how did you remember that? That is so awesome, that you would remember."

"I haven't forgotten much about you, Addy. I had to keep my pictures of you at my Mom's house after Hannah and I got married. Sometimes, I would try and picture your face and couldn't, so I'd go to my mom's place and look at you."

"There's someone I want you to meet, Frankie."

"Your son, I imagine."

"Yes, he should be awake from his nap by now, I'll go upstairs and get him."

"Why don't you stay off your ankle? I'll go get him, where is he?"

"Second door on the left, in the hallway."

He went up the stairs and came back down, holding onto Robbie's hand as they descended the stairs. When they got to the bottom, the boy ran to his mother.

"Robbie," she said, "I want you to meet a good friend of Mommy's. Say hello to Mister Frankie."

"I go by Frank now, Addy. I figured it was time to become an adult. Only my mother calls me Frankie anymore."

"Oh, okay, Frank," she said. "I have no problem with that. Say hello to Mister Frank, Robbie."

"Hello, Mister Frank," the boy said, and Frank took his hand and shook it.

"Hello to you, Robbie," Frank said, "I am really glad to meet you, but why don't you just call me Frank and drop the mister, okay?"

"Okay," he said.

"He's the same age as my Penny."

"I wanted to come to you when Daddy told me about her accident, but I was afraid it would complicate things for you. I prayed for Penny every day, still do. I want to meet her."

"She's at your dad's house," he said. "Your dad pulled a fast one on me, he sent me to pick up a couple of things."

"He meant me and Robbie."

"Oh, right. I didn't think of that. Are you ready to go?"

"Yes, as soon as I get Robbie's bag. We're staying at Dad and Sarah's house next week. It's spring break. Robbie, please go upstairs and get your bag."

The boy headed up the stairs. Addy took Frank's head in her hands and placed her lips on his. They kissed lovingly until they heard Robbie coming back down the stairs.

"Thank you," Frank said.

"I want more of that," she replied.

"Okay," he said, smiling broadly at her.

They drove toward New Roads and, when they got to Riverbend, Frank pulled of the highway onto the property.

"Right here, Addy, is where my mother told your dad she would marry him."

"You would not believe how happy she has made him."

"Oh, yeah, I would. I do know. It's fun to watch them together. They are really happy."

"He loved her half his life before they finally found each other. Can you imagine, or conceive of a man loving a woman that long, always hoping she will become his wife, one day?" Addy said, marveling at that thought.

"Uh, yeah, Addy, I can," Frank said. "I fell in love with you when I was fifteen, and I'll be thirty-one in six months."

Clay and Sarah made dinner that night. Frankie and Addy sat next to each other, and Robbie and Penny sat across the table from them.

Frank raised his glass and tapped it with his knife to get everyone's attention.

"Mister Connor, I am in love with your daughter and, with your permission, I wish to ask her to marry me."

"Well, Frank, you let me marry your mother, so I think it's only fair that I let you marry my daughter, as long as she consents, that is."

"I consent," Addy said, raising her hand.

The wedding took place in the Connor backyard, at the same spot where Clay and Sarah were married. Father Murphy was away on sabbatical, so a young priest filled in for him. Bill Packer was able to understand what the new priest was saying.

Bobby Soutullo was Frank's best man, and Penny Ross was Addy's maid of honor.

Clay offered to pay for them to honeymoon in Paris, but they declined. "We just want to borrow the boat, Daddy," Addy said. "I didn't tell you everything, Frank," Addy told him.

"You're holding out on me, and you tell me now, after we're married?"

"I'm sorry, it slipped my mind. You see, Rob went to prison for doing illegal business. It's not important that you know what he did. Suffice it to say, he went to prison, he's still there. But Rob's dad was a real sweetheart to me after all the trouble. Dan, that's Rob's dad, bought me a new car and gave me the house that Rob and I were living in. He sold the house, recently, and deposited the money into my bank account."

"Okay, am I supposed to ask?"

"Ask what?"

"How much money it is?"

"Well, I thought I should tell you. I want to build us a house on the river with a boat dock and boat house, just like Dad and Sarah's house."

"Holy cow, Addy, maybe I should ask how much money you have."

"I have two-million-dollars, Frank." He just looked at her, stupefied, and she started laughing. "Well, go ahead, say something. You aren't mad, are you?"

"So, you're telling me I married a rich woman? No, Addy, I'm not mad."

"I still want to teach school. Are you still okay with that."

"Yes, Addy, I'm okay with you teaching school. I'm pretty much okay with anything you want to do."

Sarah Ross Connor and Addy Connor Ross would be a lasting blessing to the little town in which they grew up and became happy women. The people of the town went on, living, loving, and talking about each other. Larry Moran received the death penalty for murdering Eve Cormier, and Beau Woodley was sentenced to life without parole. Captain Will Harmon was there when Moran was put to sleep.

Martin Aucoin never told a soul about Clay Connor's helping Frankie Ross get loans, to start his business and to do the large apartment complex in Baton Rouge.

There were rumors going around that Morris Hebert had been seen leaving Louise Cormier's house, just before daybreak, on several occasions. But the rumors were never confirmed, and it was speculated that, had Louise or Morris been asked, they would have denied the accusations.

Louise Cormier turned out to be an astute and responsible business woman. She ran Justin's business as well as he had, and the company morale seemed to thrive under her tutelage. Morris Hebert was promoted to general manager and profits continued to set records, despite the fact that they no longer sold dope across the neighboring parishes to Point Coupee.

Addy Ross became a school teacher, at the local Catholic High School, and loved Frank Ross forever. And Frank Ross loved her back. They built their house on the River and lived there the rest of their lives. True love is not bound by time, it is a prisoner only of the heart.

The world was in turmoil, with wars and rumors of wars, all over the globe. Human beings were in contentious conflict, everywhere, evidenced by the evening news and the morning papers. But on this night, as the sun gently set, on the beautiful lake, known as False River, then moved out of the way, allowing a haloed moon to contend with the darkness.

All was well, In New Roads, Louisiana.

End of Story

About the Author

Jack Sprouse is from Dallas, Texas, although he now lives in Lewisville, a few miles north of Dallas. He studied American History at Texas Tech, in Lubbock, and his fields of greatest historical interest are the American Civil War and World War II. He served in the United States Navy as a crewmember on an ASW (anti-submarine-warfare) patrol aircraft. Writing fiction is his passion.

Sprouse just loves making stuff up (his mom used to punish him for doing that when he was a kid). He has written two books of historical fiction: *Adventures in Time Book I: The American Civil War* and *Adventures in Time Book II: The American West.* These are both Walter Mitty type stories in which he places himself back in time as a war correspondent following historical events and interviewing the major players in those events; two books of original poetry, *The Quiet Place* and *Dreams of a Forgotten Man.* Both books contain approximately fifty original poems on various subjects: Life, love, friendship, relationships, war, conflict, tragedy; and several novels: *The House Wren*, a saga of a fictional Texas family; *On Nep-*

tune Wings, a love story set in the 1960s against the backdrop of a US Navy Patrol Squadron; *Magnolia Road*, an improbable love story between a girl from Vermont and a rancher from Colorado. She is purposeful and dedicated to her chosen calling in life; and *Clare*, about a 24-year-old woman who faces life with quiet confidence and inner turmoil; experiencing love, hurt, uncertainty, sexual harassment in the workplace, and tragedy. He is currently working on several ideas for new books.

www.ingramcontent.com/pod-product-compliance
Lightning Source LLC
Chambersburg PA
CBHW072220170626
46813CB00003B/1031